David Miller Barbour

**The Silver Crisis**

India's financial and commercial sufferings

David Miller Barbour

**The Silver Crisis**
*India's financial and commercial sufferings*

ISBN/EAN: 9783337378554

Printed in Europe, USA, Canada, Australia, Japan

Cover: Foto ©Andreas Hilbeck / pixelio.de

More available books at **www.hansebooks.com**

# The Silver Crisis.

———◆——

# INDIA'S FINANCIAL AND COMMERCIAL SUFFERINGS.

## LETTER BY

# Sir David Barbour, K.C.S.I.

*(Finance Minister to the Indian Government).*

*Published 23rd August, 1892.*

MANCHESTER :
J. E. CORNISH, ST. ANN'S SQUARE.

LONDON:
EFFINGHAM WILSON, ROYAL EXCHANGE.

# REMARKABLE PREDICTION IN 1871.
## VERIFIED IN 1892.

——:·:——

The following remarkable prediction, by the late Mr. Ernest Seyd, in 1871, as to the effects of the demonetisation of Silver—two years before Germany (previously Silver) and the United States of America (previously Bimetallic) changed to a Gold Standard of Value, and the Latin Union stopped the unrestricted coinage of Silver—will be read with much interest in view of its confirmation by the current events of to-day:

"It is a great mistake to suppose that the adoption of the gold valuation by other States besides England will be beneficial. It will only lead to the destruction of the monetary equilibrium hitherto existing, and cause a fall in the value of Silver, from which England's trade and the Indian Silver valuation will suffer more than all other interests, grievous as the general decline of prosperity all over the world will be."

"The strong doctrinism existing in England as regards the gold valuation is so blind that, when the time of depression sets in, there will be this special feature:—The economical authorities of the country will refuse to listen to the cause here fore-shadowed; every possible attempt will be made to prove that the decline of commerce is due to all sorts of causes and irreconcilable matters. The workman and his strikes will be the first convenient target; then speculation and over-trading will have their turn. Later on, when foreign nations, unable to pay in silver, have recourse to protection, when a number of other secondary causes develop themselves; then many would-be wise men will have the opportunity of pointing to specific reasons which in their eyes account for the falling off in every branch of trade. Many other allegations will be' made totally irrelevant to the real issue, but satisfactory to the moralising tendency of financial writers. The great danger of the time will then be that, among all this confusion and strife, England's supremacy in commerce and manufactures may go backwards to an extent which cannot be redressed, when the real cause becomes recognised, and the natural remedy is applied."

# THE SILVER CRISIS

AND

# INDIA.

*Reprinted from the "TIMES," August 23rd, 1892.*

TO THE EDITOR OF THE "TIMES."

Sir,—May I ask your insertion of the enclosed letter, which I have just received from Sir David Barbour, and which I think is of sufficient public interest at the present to justify my request.— Yours, &c.,

W. H. HOULDSWORTH.

Coodham, Kilmarnock, N.B., Aug. 19, 1892.

---

"Simla, India, July 25th, 1892.

"My dear Houldsworth,—It is nearly four years since we parted in London, and it occurs to me that you may like to know how the experience of the last four years, during which I have been in charge of the Indian finances, has affected my opinions on the currency question.

"On that point I can give you a very decided answer. I have no hesitation in saying that a common standard of value for England and India is absolutely essential for the well-being of this country, and that by far the best and safest method of attaining so desirable a result is, to the best of my judgment, the adoption of the system of double legal tender by international agreement.

"The continuance of the present state of things is ruinous to Indian interest; the fluctuations in exchange affect our foreign trade most injuriously; the theory that the evil effects of such fluctuations can be eliminated by the exchange banks is not supported by facts. For example, a merchant in Calcutta may simultaneously buy piece goods in Manchester, sell them in India, and fix his exchange, but if exchange rises, say, 20 per cent before the goods are paid for in India the Indian purchaser finds that others can import the same goods 20 per cent cheaper, and undersell him to that extent.

"In such case the Indian trader either suffers a ruinous loss, or he breaks his engagement and refuses to take delivery.

"I enclose copy of a petition by native traders in Kurrachee, which shows how seriously they feel the evils from which we suffer.* And I may say generally, that merchants and bankers in India are very much disheartened and thoroughly dissatisfied.

"The extent to which their opinions have turned in favour of bimetallism is remarkable, though on the Bombay side there is a strong party in favour of maintaining the status quo in consequence of the belief they entertain that a silver standard and a falling rupee give them an advantage over Lancashire.

"But, unfortunately, this conversion to a belief in bimetallism is accompanied with a feeling of helplessness, as it is feared that the opposition of England will stand in the way of a satisfactory international agreement.

"On this account many men in India begin to contemplate the establishment of a gold standard, arguing, I believe, that the gold standard would either prove a remedy for the evils from which they suffer or that it would produce a state of things which would force on international bimetallism.

"The effect on Indian finance of the want of a common standard with the rest of the Empire is deplorable. In the estimates of the current year I had to provide for an additional charge of 1,700,000Rx. on account of the fall in exchange; for next year I anticipate a further charge of 1,500,000Rx.

"If there is a surplus I am afraid to recommend the remission of taxation, as a week may see the surplus dis-

* See copy of Petition, p. 12.

appear. If there is a deficit I cannot propose taxation, as a turn of the wheel may convert a deficit into a surplus.

"In public, as in private finance, such a state of things produces a certain amount of recklessness which is not favourable to economy. Whether we are economical or the reverse, the question of a surplus or a deficit depends not on any action of ours, but rather on the course of exchange, and the course of exchange depends on we know not what.

"There are many thousands of miles of railway that might be made in India with great advantage to the country, which would at once return a moderate rate of interest on the capital, and which would ultimately pay well. The fear of a fall in silver, however, stands in the way of their construction. If it was probable that these railways would return a large percentage of profit at once, they would no doubt be constructed whatever the Indian standard of value might be, but with the small, though certain, profit which Indian railways are likely to return for the first few years the risk of investing capital in a country with a silver standard deters the prudent investor, while such railways have no attraction for the more speculative.

" Meanwhile English capital flows into fraudulent companies, and is lent to foreign states where bankruptcy is only a question of time.

" It is an uphill fight which you have before you, but the principles of bimetallism have made great, though quiet, progress, and perhaps the reform may come more quickly than we now anticipate.

" It used to be said that the Europeans in India merely wanted two shillings for their rupee. It was an ungenerous taunt at the best of times, and it is certainly not true in the present day. Almost any ratio between gold and silver would be gladly accepted if it were only permanent and stable.—I remain, yours very truly,

(Signed)     " D. BARBOUR.

" Sir W. H. Houldsworth, Bart., M.P."

The letter which we print to-day from Sir David Barbour
on the monetary and commercial crisis in India will attract
widespread attention, and cannot fail to produce a profound
impression in the controversy on the currency question.
Sir David Barbour has been nearly thirty years in India,
serving for a considerable portion of the time as Financial
Secretary, while, during the last four years, he has occupied
the position of Finance Minister with distinguished ability.
Our readers will also remember that he was one of the most
prominent members of the Royal Commission on Gold and
Silver. Few men, indeed, speak with equal weight upon
the monetary question generally, and as regards its application to India he is undoubtedly the greatest authority of the
day. From his position it is perhaps natural that he should
more particularly have regard to the effects of a low and
fluctuating exchange upon India; but seeing how large our
trade is with that portion of the Empire, and that owing
to hostile tariffs we shall probably have to rely more and
more upon the free markets of the East as an outlet for our
manufactures, it requires no arguments to demonstrate that
what materially affects India bears directly upon our prosperity. It will, therefore, arrest the serious attention of all
engaged in manufacturing for the Eastern markets to learn
that in Sir David's opinion a continuance of the present
dislocated system of currency—part of the Empire being on
a gold standard and part on a silver standard—without any
stable par of exchange between the two moneys, is simply
ruinous to the interests of India. A favourite contention of
those who take a superficial view of the situation is that the
evils of a fluctuating exchange can always be overcome by
means of a contract with an Exchange bank. Sir David
shows by a simple illustration that this is a complete fallacy,
and the troubles which have long been experienced by those

engaged in the ordinary way of trade with the East will fully confirm his opinion.

No one trading on 'Change in Manchester can be in any doubt as to this. The manufacturer has had bitter experience that even a slight alteration in the exchange checks business; and of late the fluctuation has been so great that trade may almost be said to have collapsed. Spinners and manufacturers have many spindles and looms stopped, and some of them have heavy stocks on hand, and the outlook, unless some fundamental alteration can be effected, seems cheerless in the extreme. Sir David Barbour gives little hope of any improvement in India. Its foreign trade is being "most injuriously affected" by the exchange fluctuations, while their effect on the finances of our Dependency is "deplorable." He mentions that for the current year he has had to provide for an additional charge, as compared with last year, of 17,000,000 rupees on account of the fall in exchange, and anticipates a further charge of 15,000,000 rupees for next year. He also shows that the Indian Government cannot with prudence remit taxation, however favourable the financial outlook may be, and therefore the people of India have to be taxed practically to the extremest limit so long as the present system obtains. One very important point affecting not only the textile industry, but also the iron and steel trade, is that referring to the construction, or rather non-construction, of railways in India. We have more than once drawn pointed attention to this, but we have it now on the authority of the Finance Minister, that " many thousands of miles of railways might " be made in India with great advantage to the country, " which would return a moderate rate of interest on the " capital, and which would ultimately pay well," but " the " fear of a fall in silver stands in the way of their construc- " tion." We also know that not only has the flow of British capital to India stopped, but the tide is now running the other way, and many investments with the Indian banks are being withdrawn, a course which must still further cripple trade. That the position of affairs calls for a remedy no one now will dare to deny. During the course of the recent discussion in the Manchester Chamber of Commerce, a policy of "drift" was really the only alternative propounded to Sir William Houldsworth's resolution, but, as we then predicted, such course could only end in disaster, and that eventuality is now at our doors. India is speaking out with no uncertain sound. The recently formed Indian Currency Association, which embraces many of the most prominent English and native merchants and exporters, have held a series of public meetings throughout India, at which resolutions have been passed representing the desperate condition of affairs, financial and commercial, and urging the Government to take immediate steps to provide a remedy, or the issue will be disastrous. At many of these meetings the full programme of the Currency Association has been endorsed. That programme sets forth that the best and most effective remedy is a Joint Gold and Silver Standard by an agreement amongst the nations, in which the United Kingdom and India shall be joined,* or if that should prove to be impossible, then a Gold Standard for India; and the press throughout the Dependency now generally support the demands of the association.

As will be seen, Sir David Barbour unhesitatingly declares that "the best and safest" remedy for the admitted evils is an International Joint Gold and Silver Standard, and he speaks of the great change of public opinion in India in favour of Bimetallism. It is interesting to note in passing his remarks with regard to opinion in Bombay. There opinion is somewhat divided, as some believe "a silver

*Extract from the Petition of the Indian Currency Association to the House of Commons :—" Your petitioners represent that the introduction of the double standard can only be effected by international arrangement, but that international concert has hitherto been found impossible ; that another international Conference is now about to meet ; that it is of the most vital importance to the interests of the Government and people of this Empire that an agreement should be arrived at ; and that, therefore, every effort should be used on behalf of India to secure its success."

"standard and a falling rupee give them an advantage "over Lancashire," while it will be remembered that some of the opponents of Sir William Houldsworth's resolution on the currency question in our Chamber of Commerce actually urged that a low exchange is of advantage to Lancashire. The feeling of "helplessness" which in India accompanies the desire for bimetallism is not difficult to understand. They judge English public opinion largely through what they see in the London press, and on this subject, with scarcely an exception, the daily and also the weekly financial press of the metropolis absolutely misrepresent that opinion. Many important public facts bearing on the movement in favour of bimetallism are rigorously ignored. They seriously put forward "arguments" which would make even a student of monetary science, who is possessed of intelligence, blush, and it is an "open secret" that most of them mercilessly basket any correspondence sent pointing out their errors of commission or omission. Those who intelligently regard the signs of the times, however, know that the movement in this country in favour of monetary reform is a factor which has to be reckoned with the interests of the great productive industries of this country, upon which the masses of the people depend for their support, must be paramount, and manufacturers and the wage-earning classes are now in such numbers advocating international bimetallism that no Government can disregard the demand. The International Monetary Conference, which will meet in a few weeks, will deal with an issue of the gravest import to this country and India, and we trust that no opportunity will be lost of backing up the Indian demand by demonstrating how earnest is the desire here also to have a stable exchange between the two great moneys of the world. We do not propose here to discuss the pros and cons of a gold standard for India—a proposal fraught with grave dangers. It is enough to know that the Government and the great mass of the commercial world in India put forward international bimetallism as the first and best remedy, and that it is also required by the most important and the most numerous class in this country—labour employing capitalists and wage earners—while the highest authorities in political economy in this and other countries endorse its theory and pronounce it orthodox.

---

*Leading Article reprinted from the* "MANCHESTER GUARDIAN," *Tuesday, August 23rd, 1892.*

The interesting and important letter from Sir David Barbour, the Minister of Finance for India, which we publish elsewhere, ought to put an end to much controversy as to the interests of India in regard to the Silver Question. One statement in the letter will deservedly attract attention in Lancashire. That India as a whole is rapidly getting into line with Lancashire in peremptorily demanding that "the policy of drift" shall be abandoned has been apparent for some time past to observers of Indian affairs and Indian opinion, and the rapid progress of the new Indian Currency Association has now put the practical unanimity of the demand beyond question. But much has been made of the fact that the Bombay Chamber of Commerce has not repealed a resolution against any interference passed six years ago by that body. The opponents of the bimetallist memorial recently adopted by the Manchester Chamber of Commerce quoted the Bombay Chamber's old decision as an argument, and special prominence has since been given to it by some of Lancashire's critics in London. Sir David Barbour now fully endorses the explanation of the hesitancy of the members of the Bombay Chamber which has previously been given in our columns. It was due, he says, to a belief that "a falling rupee gives them an advantage over Lancashire." The reference is, of course, to the Bombay millowners; and the belief is so far justified that, after an exhaustive investigation some years ago into the circumstances of the Bombay and Lancashire cotton spinning and weaving industries, the Manchester Chamber of Commerce arrived at the conclusion that every fall in the gold price of the rupee does give the Bombay millowner an artificial advantage over his Lancashire competitor. And this is obvious, for the Bombay producer, working on a rupee basis, need not advance the rupee prices of his goods when the gold exchange falls, whereas the Lancashire exporter must increase the rupee price or sell at a loss until he gets his adjustments, which only come after a long time and are never more than partial. The contention has been proved over and over again. Now Sir David Barbour shows us that, while the fall of exchange helps the establishment of a really exotic industry in India, the whole wages fund of which is relatively insignificant, it vitally injures every real Indian interest. The foreign trade of India as a whole is reduced, as the Kurrachee and Bengal native producers and merchants have urged, to mere gambling; the utter uncertainty of the position encourages a spirit of recklessness even in public departments; all attempts to adjust taxation to the necessary requirements of the administration become futile; and British capital is shut out from India, where it might be profitably invested, to the advantage of ourselves and our Indian fellow-subjects. It may be pointed out, as an illustration of the dangerous unsoundness of the existing conditions, that merely during the time which it has taken to convey his letter from Simla Sir David's estimate of the additional loss to the Government by exchange this year has become quite erroneous, as the further drop which has meanwhile taken place makes it probable that the amount will be at least double what he calculated barely more than three weeks ago. The Home Government cannot afford to neglect a question which is involving consequences of such serious import to the prosperity of India and to the very existence of the great industries of this country.

*Karachi, June 27th, 1892.*

To

# H. E. M. JAMES, Esq., C.S.,

*Commissioner in Sind.*

### The Humble Memorial of the Native Traders of Karachi.

SHOWETH,

We Native Traders of Karachi born and bred to trade exclusively and having no other calling, are now in process of discovering that our occupation is likely to vanish altogether, unless something can be done to make the value of the money by which our trade is carried on permanent, or at least to free it from the violent and unintelligible fluctuations to which it is now apparently always subject.

You are aware that for the last three months we have in self defence been compelled to combine to cease purchasing European commodities in our customary way. For this reason, that the moderate profit which we look to make we have found altogether inadequate to cover the risks and losses to which we are subjected by the constant change in the value of the Rupee.

When we bought Manchester Grey Cloth two years ago on a basis of 1/4½ exchange, we could have no idea that a loss of about 15 per cent. by the sudden rise in exchange would be inflicted upon us by causes altogether outside the normal fluctuations of our local market and over which we had no control; nor could we have anticipated the causes which brought ruin to us through contracts we had entered into with Exporting Firms for wheat and seeds, when the Rupee was valued at 1,8 in English money. Then, as we say, the value of the Rupee stood at 1s. 8d., but when we came to carry out these contracts its value had fallen to 1s. 6d., and we found that in consequence we had to provide more Rupees with which to buy the produce to fulfil our contracts than we had agreed to take from the Exporting Firms.

To illustrate the risk we are subjected to we have only to draw your attention to the fluctuations of the present month.

On the 2nd Exchange was 1/3$\frac{1}{16}$.

On the 9th Exchange was 1/3$\frac{11}{16}$ giving a rise of 4½ per cent.

On the 16th Exchange was 1/3$\frac{1}{4}$ giving a fall of 1½ per cent.

On the 23rd Exchange was 1/3$\frac{7}{8}$ giving a further fall of 2½ per cent.

What it will be to-morrow and whether for loss or profit to us we cannot say.

The hardship of our position is intensified by the fact that we can in no way protect ourselves from these losses, because, while we may sell with the knowledge we have of up-country supplies to Exporting Firms, it is impossible for us to buy against our contracts till the produce collected in small quantities in the districts is brought to market, and it is in this interval that the constant changing in the value of the Rupee turns our legitimate trading transactions from safe business to purely speculative gambling.

It is this which makes us fear that unless some means can be found to give steadiness of value to the Rupee, let it be high or low but steady, which will enable us as in days gone by to calculate with some certainty the result of our transactions, an absolute destruction of our trade must sooner or later overtake us.

We therefore beg that you will be graciously pleased to make a representation to Government urging the essential need of some steps being taken to put a stop to the intolerable uncertainty as to the value of the Rupee.

And we will as in duty bound ever pray.—

# SILVER AND INDIAN FINANCE

By SAMUEL MONTAGU, M.P.

*Reprinted from* "THE FORTNIGHTLY REVIEW," *October*, 1892.

LONDON:

CHAPMAN AND HALL, Ld.

So much has been written about the disturbed relations between gold and silver, we have heard so frequently of the "battle of the standards," that it requires some courage to go into the arena, especially to espouse the weaker cause.

In recording a few arguments in favour of silver it is not intended to discuss the whole subject of bimetallism, and the decline in prices its cessation has caused, but to submit some reasons against allowing silver to sink to depths unknown, with consequent disaster to India, and to traders with silver-using countries.

It has been urged that a decline in the price of the white metal will restrict its production; but there can be no certainty of such a result, because silver is largely a by-product, and costs but little to separate from lead and other metals. Besides, in mining the precious metals, we have to reckon with the speculative spirit which forces on the work so long as there is any money to spend. It is doubtful whether there is a case on record in which a gold or silver mining company has been wound up, and a substantial portion of its capital has been returned to the shareholders.

Now let us consider the present situation from a practical business point of view. Is it not a fact that we overrate the importance of the actual gold circulation in this country? It cannot reach a hundred million sterling, whereas our general assets are to be reckoned in thousands of millions.

Speaking on the score of convenience, it would be easier to dispense with gold than with silver. Banknotes down to a pound could be issued, and silver used for small payments. The circulating medium has, however, a twofold duty to perform; it ought not only to pass easily from hand to hand in our own country, but should also be available to liquidate our indebtedness abroad. Gold can pay our debts in Europe, in parts of America, and in some of our dependencies, but silver is required for India, China, Japan, and the Straits Settlements. It is therefore essential to ensure a sufficient supply of gold and silver for all our requirements.

The great burden of regulating the gold value of silver and rendering it stable is too heavy for any one, or even for any two countries, and the fiasco in the United States, which was foreseen by English financiers, is unjustly quoted as an argument against universal bimetallism, whereas bimetallists think that their system will be adopted through the very disaster impending in America.

Every country in the world has an interest in silver, and a proposal made by this country for an International Convention for at least twenty years, fixing a reasonable ratio between gold and silver, ought to find universal acceptance.

A very short sketch of a plan submitted by me to my colleagues on the Royal Gold and Silver Commission is annexed, and will give sufficient technical detail. This article, however, being intended for the general public who are unacquainted with the subject, it may be of service to attempt here a simple explanation of that apparently complex subject, bimetallism.

Bimetallism means the practically free coinage of gold and silver for the public, and making the gold and silver thus coined full legal tender for the discharge of all debts. For instance, at our Mint any one bringing an ounce of standard gold ($\frac{11}{12}$ fine) would receive in return £3 17s. 10½d. The law might be extended to silver, so that any one bringing to the Mint twenty ounces of silver of standard quality would receive also £3 17s. 10½d. A slight deduction might properly be made to cover the bare cost of coining. The owner of the proceeds of his ounce of gold, or twenty ounces of silver, could then pay away with equal facility either the gold or the silver to any one in the United Kingdom. Bimetallism practically prevailed over the whole world until 1873, inasmuch as silver could be readily exchanged for gold, and *vice versâ*, in France and Germany. Thus this country enjoyed until that date all the advantages of bimetallism, minus the cost of freight, &c., in effecting the required exchanges on the Continent, the principal advantage being the fairly stable condition of the exchanges with silver-using countries.

Should bimetallism be established in this country, no appreciable change or disturbance in our habits and customs would ensue; no increase in our silver circulation need take place; payment would be made as now, either by cheque or banknotes; no one would attempt to annoy his neighbour by paying him an inconvenient sum in silver coin, any more than he would do now in gold coin. Shopkeepers and other traders would then, as now, pay silver and gold into their bankers, paying away cheques drawn against the amount so paid in by them.

The bankers would suffer no further inconvenience than at present, probably even less, for under a bimetallic *régime* the Bank of England would readily accept both silver and gold, whereas, now, silver coin in large quantities is frequently refused by the Bank of England.

Now let us shortly consider the arguments advanced against bimetallism. It is sometimes asserted that bimetallism is impossible. We need only reply that the members of the Royal Commission on Gold and Silver, although equally divided as to its advisability, were agreed as to its practicability.

It is then urged that bimetallism has failed on the continent of Europe and in the United States. To that argument we would submit the reply that the system only came to an end in France and the adjoining countries on account of unwillingness to help Germany in the absurd desire to demonetize her silver. In the United States it has failed because bimetallism must be almost general, otherwise the pioneer country will lose the metal most preferred by others.

For argument's sake, let us suppose that the countries comprised in the Latin Union and the United States introduced effective bimetallism (the United States has coined hitherto only silver tokens), while England and Germany stood outside the Convention. The result would be that investors would prefer to hold the securities of, or keep their money in, England or Germany, so that they could be sure of gold in case they desired that metal.

Should, however, all the great Powers enter into a Bimetallic Convention, with identical mint regulations, gold would lose its present pre-eminence ; no advantage would be derived by its selection for exportation, because in every country it would have exactly the same relation to silver, and have absolutely no premium. In fact, gold would be the more plentiful metal on account of the release of gold by the national banks and treasuries, where it is now jealously hoarded. On the other hand, silver being desired by Eastern populations, who are too poor for a gold circulation, silver would be in demand for commercial enterprise in silver-using countries. It has been urged that the world's enormous stock of gold would be gradually absorbed for the arts. The inference is utterly fallacious, because in the course of time so large a quantity of old jewellery, watch-cases, &c., would be received from the public that the quantity of fresh gold absorbed would tend to diminish rather than to increase. It is further said that we could not get all the great Powers to join in such a Convention, and if we did there would be the risk of one or more breaking the contract.

As to the first part of the objection, bimetallists desire no more in the first instance than that such a proposal should be made. The introduction of the bimetallic system depends, of course, upon the general adherence of the Powers. The second assumed difficulty may be met by the fact that international conventions for postal and telegraphic facilities have never been broken ; therefore equally unreasonable is it to suppose that any great Power would break a financial convention, by which, in fact, the offending country could only lose.

This question, however, is frequently put : Supposing one of the countries in the Bimetallic Convention suspended specie payments, how then? In such a case gold and silver would leave that country, and be distributed all over the world, until the resumption of specie payments took place.

One question continually cropping up is: If you can fix internationally a ratio between gold and silver of 20 to 1, what is to prevent it being fixed at 15½ to 1, or even at 10 to 1?

To this the evident reply is that, as we have to deal with human beings full of prejudice and sentiment, if we unduly enhance the price of silver by establishing an unreasonable ratio, we shall create an expectation of an ultimate termination of the Bimetallic Convention, and thus induce the hoarding of gold. On the other hand, if all the great Powers entered into a Convention fixing a reasonable ratio between gold and silver, the result would be that gold would be much more plentiful, as it would no longer be hoarded by national banks.

The final important objection raised is that bimetallism would greatly encourage the production of silver, and the world would be deluged with that metal, although such a result could not occur if a reasonable ratio be fixed. I would ask, What possible disaster would result? How would it be in the case of gold? Is not its production beneficial through the distribution of wealth? Surely if the ratio were fixed at 20 to 1 it would be equally beneficial if either 20,000,000 ounces of silver were produced, or 1,000,000 ounces of gold.

Gold is naturally enhanced in value by being used for currency purposes. Why should silver be excluded from full circulation, seeing that by depriving that metal of its main use you artificially diminish its value?

Now what dangers would be prevented and what advantages would be conferred by bimetallism? These are the essential points, for, unless it can be shown that great dangers would be averted and that great advantages would result, it would obviously be unwise to advocate a change.

The first, perhaps the chief advantage, would accrue to India, where many hundreds of millions sterling circulate in silver, which will ultimately have but little international value if bimetallism be not re-established. The financial position of our great dependency is already endangered by the great decline in the gold value of the rupee, because India's chief indebtedness to England is in gold, and the fall of 1d. in the rupee entails the annual loss of over £1,000,000; consequently the decline from 2s. which has already occurred imposes an additional burden on India of over £9,000,000 per annum. The bulk of India's Government and railway debt was incurred when the rupee was at least 50 per cent. higher than at present; the decline in the value of the rupee entails an ever-growing burden on the Indian taxpayer.

This condition of affairs may not be without compensation, in the shape of increased production in India, and in larger exports to this country; but all will admit that the uncertainty as to the future must be an anxiety of the gravest character to the Government of India. Consequently any efficient means of giving stability to the rupee would be of the greatest advantage.

When a country is cursed with an inconvertible paper currency trade suffers from the constant fluctuations in the outside exchanges, and every effort is made to revert to specie payments, even at a great sacrifice. England passed through such a trial less than a hundred years ago; so, also, have France, the United States, and Italy; yet an inconvertible paper currency is less injurious than is a silver currency at the present time. A Government can regulate the issue of their paper; this can be controlled and kept within the requirements of circulation; no outside influence can increase its volume, while the expectation of redemption tends to prevent undue depreciation of its paper currency in a well-governed country.

Greenbacks, issued in the United States by Abraham Lincoln, were at one time at over 40 per cent. discount. They were humorously likened to the children of Israel, being the issue of Abraham, and knowing no redeemer. But events have shown that this was a mistake; they have been redeemed, and for years past have been on a par with gold. Now silver in India can be indefinitely increased from outside; all the world pours into that country the silver which cannot be used elsewhere, and cannot be again exported from India.

If our great dependency ceased to receive silver, the fall in its price would be enormous, but if India tried to export silver, no country would have it even at half its actual gold price. Thus a great mass of silver, valued even at present prices at hundreds of millions sterling, would have little international value.

The difficulty of exacting revenue by fresh taxation in India would make any fixed bimetallic ratio welcome as a relief from probable danger of a most serious political and financial character. An alternative remedy has been suggested, namely, establishing a gold currency in India, and agitation in its favour is increasing in India itself. Our Government will, no doubt, be called upon before long to make a choice between one or the other method of giving stability to the rupee.

If one of our great self-governing colonies were in such a position, a decision would be promptly forced upon us.

The evil effects resulting from the depreciation of silver have been sufficiently proved by the evidence submitted to the Royal Commission, and all admit the benefit of having a stable currency between different parts of our Empire. The united opinion of the

Commissioners was to the effect that bimetallism was possible, and that as a cure for these ever-recurring difficulties it held the field, no other remedy being able to approach it in effectiveness.

On the other hand, if we adopt the alternative proposal, and close our Indian mints against the free coinage of silver for the public, let us not shut our eyes to the difficulties which stand in the way. Some friction would in consequence be created with native Indian mints, especially where we exercise insufficient control, as well as with those of our subjects who live close to the Chinese frontier of India. The trade between India and China and Japan would be seriously affected, because the decline of silver would no longer drag down the gold price of the rupee; all Indian manufactures, including opium, would apparently rise in silver-using countries.

Such an Act would, by reducing its employment as coin, necessarily cause a further heavy decline in silver, resulting probably in a panic in India, which could, however, be somewhat allayed by purchases of silver by the Government in India (somewhat after the fashion which now obtains in the United States) by inviting public tenders of that metal for coinage.

The apparent profit on coining by the Indian Government could be applied in reduction of the public debt. It should not be dealt with as has been the case in this country, where, during the last six years, nearly £2,000,000, the apparent profit on coining silver, has been treated as revenue and spent. That money was in reality borrowed without interest, and must eventually be repaid, and even exceeded, in the withdrawal of worn coin. Besides, our Australian colonies are clamouring to participate in the profit of issuing this debased currency.

In the meantime we have in circulation throughout the Empire about £25,000,000 nominal value of English silver—the actual gold value of which cannot now exceed £13,000,000, leaving a difference of £12,000,000 for posterity to deal with.

In passing from this subject it would be as well to mention that silver, which during many years before 1872 varied but slightly from 60d. per ounce, was coined into silver token money at 66d., a profit of about 10 per cent., in order to prevent its export as bullion. Owing to the decline of silver to 38d., the apparent profit on coining our silver is nearly 75 per cent., and in consequence of its worn condition the gold value of the £25,000,000 can only be estimated at about £13,000,000, each shilling being worth little over sixpence.

One result of this enormous difference between the uncoined metal and our silver tokens is the fraudulent coining of half-crowns, florins, and shillings in good silver, which imitations circulate with complete immunity to the forger, no one outside the Mint and, perhaps, the Bank of England being able to detect such illegal token money.

International bimetallism would lessen this danger, which threatens almost every country where the silver currency is coined at the old value of 60d., although the danger is greater in our country, where we continue to coin at 66d. per ounce standard.

It will suffice to mention one more great advantage which would result from international bimetallism. Capital is at present very abundant, mainly owing to depression of trade, coupled with low prices for all staples. It would be of immense benefit if we could safely invest our superabundant capital in silver-using countries. Commercial enterprises in India, China, and Japan would revive trade, and bring renewed prosperity to the commercial and working classes. But would any prudent merchant change his gold into the currencies of those great countries under the present condition of silver ? The enormous losses already incurred during the last twenty years through the decline in the gold value of silver are sufficient to kill all legitimate trading by Englishmen in those countries.

If it be urged that our chief concern is within our own Empire, let us in any case endeavour to give stability to the gold value of the rupee. The only thoroughly effective mode is international bi-metallism, and I venture to assert that, if all the great Powers were to enter into such a convention, on a plan similar to the one annexed, no opponent of bimetallism could give an instance of a concrete transaction in the exchange of gold and silver, which would inflict upon this country loss or even inconvenience.

The approaching monetary conference is, perhaps, the last chance of averting the greatest danger which has ever threatened our Indian Empire.

Let not our Government palter with this question ; let them decide on one of the courses open to us : let our delegates be instructed to act decisively at that conference. If it is to be international bimetallism, with all the great Powers engaged to fix a reasonable ratio between gold and silver, so be it. The question would be settled for the duration of the convention, possibly for all time. If that measure is considered to be of too drastic a character, let us announce our intention of closing the Indian mints to the coinage of silver for the public. The result would be that the Council of India could sell their bills, say, at at least 1s. 4d. per rupee, without lessening exports from India.

No doubt more remittances would be required to pay for Indian products ; those remittances could be made in gold, the Indian Government undertaking, until further notice, to coin gold pieces of the intrinsic value of our sovereign to be legal tender for fifteen rupees, the Indian banks and the Government in India to have the option of paying out either the existing silver rupees or the new gold coins.

The consequence of such an arrangement would be that silver bars would decline still further in price, and would furnish a test of the theory of monometallists, who assert that silver production would, in that case, be so reduced that silver would find its level, and this terrible state of transition, which has imposed so heavy an incubus on trade, would terminate. Should, however, other great Powers be willing to assist the United States in re-establishing bimetallism, we should put no obstacle in the way of such a project.

The Government of the United States will most likely submit some plan to the conference; possibly they may offer some inducement under the reciprocity clauses of the McKinley Tariff, by admitting the manufactures of assenting Powers at a reduced duty. Such an offer might induce the Latin Union and Germany to help the United States out of their silver difficulty.

Should the conference prove a fiasco, there can be no doubt that the Bland Bill will be repealed, accompanied, possibly, by forced sales of silver. The United States can well afford to retrace their steps, and get rid of their accumulated silver in exchange for gold at the cost of a few millions sterling.

Are we in such a case to be unprepared? Are we to wait till bankruptcy threatens all our Indian banks, and even the Indian Government? Are we to wait till the rupee declines to 1s., or even 9d., causing widespread ruin all over the country, before taking some action in self-defence.

The three alternatives are before us, and I recapitulate them in what I deem the order of preference.

We can join all the other great Powers in establishing a reasonable ratio between gold and silver, say 20 to 1, which would maintain silver at about 47d. and the rupee at 1s. 6d. We can offer facilities to other Powers to adopt such a convention without us, by undertaking to keep the Indian mints open for the full term of that convention; by authorising the Bank of England to exercise its legal power to hold in silver a fifth of the amount it holds in gold, and by enacting that silver should be made a legal tender here up to £5 or £10. Should our Government decide against our joining a bimetallic convention, and should our endeavours to induce other Powers to adopt that system fail, we should anticipate the probable repeal of the Bland Bill, and declare our intention of closing the Indian mints against the coinage of silver for the public, as a preliminary step to the introduction of a gold currency into India.

I have endeavoured to depict as briefly as possible the dangers which threaten the Indian Government, and all engaged in trade with silver-using countries. I have suggested the means by which these dangers can be averted and commerce revived. I have tried to show that the adoption of the suggested remedies would neither injure nor inconvenience us. This most important matter must now be left in the hands of the Governments represented at the approaching conference.

---

PROPOSAL for an INTERNATIONAL CONVENTION fixing a ratio between SILVER and GOLD, submitted for the consideration of the ROYAL COMMISSION by Mr. SAMUEL MONTAGU, M.P.

1. In order to give stability to trade with silver-using countries without hindering the importation of wheat from India or unduly raising prices, it would be advisable to fix internationally the ratio at 20 to 1, a most convenient ratio, as most countries have gold coins 20 times the value of silver coins.

2. Duration of treaty should be at least 20 years.

3. The Convention should contain three conditions:—

    (a) All the contracting Governments must maintain identical mint regulations.

    (b) A mint charge should be imposed on the metal brought to the mints of (2d. an oz on gold) ½d. per oz. on silver.

    (c) Each Government must be responsible for the silver coins issued by its mints, and if at the end of, say, 19 years a year's notice be given for withdrawal from the convention, the Government so withdrawing must exchange for gold or its equivalent its silver coins existing in other countries.

4. All State Banks and the United States Treasury should be required to purchase and sell silver in the same manner as is now the case with gold ; thus there would be no actual necessity for increasing the circulation of silver.

5. With the consent of all the contracting Powers the ratio could be eventually altered to 15½ to 1.

---

Explanation as to the probable effect of the proposed Convention in the following principal countries:—

ENGLAND.

The chief importation of silver into this country would be in the form of bars, because owing to the mint charge of ½d. per oz. silver coin would be over 1 per cent. dearer than bar. If the exchange, say, at New York, showed a profit on specie remittances to this country, and if there was an available stock of bar silver obtainable at a cheaper rate than gold, which is hardly probable, as silver would usually be in special demand for India and China, silver bars would reach London as an exchange operation. Such silver would generally command a premium here over the Mint or Bank price either for immediate or future shipment to the East or to the Continent of Europe, but should there be no such demand it would be sold to the Bank in the same manner as now obtains in the case of gold. Whenever the exchanges turned against England, the silver would be bought from the Bank at, say, ₁⁄₁₆d. per oz. advance over the Bank's purchasing price, and exported instead of or equally with gold to any country to which we would be indebted. Should an increase in our silver currency be necessary, the Bank would coin the silver at the Mint into new 4s. pieces or dollars at the ratio of 20 to 1, paying the Mint the seignorage of ½d. per oz., which would have been allowed for in the Bank's purchasing price, thus bar silver would fetch at the Bank ½d. per oz. less than the value in silver coin. The existing jubilee 4s. pieces should be called in and recoined into 20 to 1 full-weight coin, which would be a full legal tender. Our token silver would circulate as at present; it would, however, be prudent to increase its weight by about 10 per cent., to prevent illegal coining with good silver. The Bank of England would issue notes against the silver held; it would be desirable that a portion of its issue should be in one-pound notes.

## FRANCE.

The French, like other Governments, would be bound by treaty not to melt down its silver coin for exportation. There would be no temptation to infringe this agreement, as the loss would be very great unless silver advanced in price through some extraordinary demand or great scarcity. If the French exchange showed a profit on specie exportations, bar silver, if any stock existed, might, as in the case of the United States, be used in the same way as gold, otherwise gold would be sent. No doubt the Bank of France would part with gold more readily after the execution of the Convention, because apprehensions of its scarcity would disappear. Silver would be the metal generally in request, owing to the great development of trade with silver-using countries. Five-franc pieces would circulate on the Continent as now; they would rest upon a more assured basis owing to the establishment of a fixed ratio.

The Bank of France would, like our Bank, purchase bar silver, and issue notes against it. In the improbable case of more silver currency being needed, a new coin could be struck, say 2½-franc pieces at 20 to 1.

## GERMANY.

Germany might be bound by treaty to coin her existing stock of bar silver, estimated at about £20,000,000, into token money, or into new four-mark pieces, at the agreed ratio of 20 to 1. The seignorage of ½d. per oz. would prevent the four-mark pieces being exported unless the country should be denuded of gold, a very improbable event. In case of war Germany would have a far larger command of gold than was the case in 1870; while silver is also useful for war purposes. In India silver alone is used.

## AMERICA.

America being a silver-producing country would be probably affected as follows :—

A mining company would generally have a better employment for silver, through orders for India and China, than at the nearest mint.

If silver currency were needed, or if orders were not forthcoming and the exchange did not permit of bullion exports, the company would coin its silver at the nearest mint, and circulate full-weight 20 to 1 now half-dollars.

The United States might call in the Bland dollars, and issue instead full-weight dollars at 20 to 1, but the Bland dollars might circulate as now as token money, like existing 5-franc pieces in France. The United States would, however, not lose much by recoining the Bland dollars, as they were coined from silver bought at low prices.

Should the exchange rise so as to admit of bullion shipments, bar silver, bar gold, or full-weight gold coin would be selected. Gold, being easier manipulated and cheaper packed, would occasionally be preferentially used. Some bar silver would be sent to England in the expectation of a premium being obtained.

It has been argued that although the minimum price of silver would under this Convention be fixed at about 47d., fluctuations might arise through a large advance in the price of silver beyond its minting price in the West, and from that advanced price variations might frequently result.

In reply to this objection it is alleged that a sufficient supply of silver would be obtained through the suspension of the Bland Act, thus releasing annually for general use about £4,000,000 of silver : also further supplies could be obtained from the existing circulation in Austria, and from those countries where silver would be coined at the new ratio of 20 to 1.

India and China could remain, as now, monometallic in silver.

The fixing a ratio of about 20 to 1 would facilitate the resumption of specie payments by Russia, Austria, and Chili.

The only serious objection which I have heard raised against this plan is, that the great Powers, especially France, would not agree to a ratio of 20 to 1, on account of the great quantity of 5-franc pieces held by the State banks, and in circulation in the countries comprised in the Latin Union.

Why should France object? She need not recoin her 5-franc pieces, for the 20 to 1 ratio would raise the price of silver to about 47d., thus rendering her silver currency more stable.

Again, the ratio of 20 to 1 would not only fix a minimum value of silver of about 47d. instead of 44d. as at present, but it would prevent the possibility of a further fall such as we have seen recently when silver dropped to 42d., whereas if no ratio be fixed silver might reach far lower depths.

As no very large quantity of silver could be had at low prices, if special demand increased or the output diminished, the old ratio of 15½ to 1 might eventually be fixed with the consent of all the contracting Powers.

RELATIVE PRICE OF SILVER TO GOLD.

Gold Standard, 916⅔/1000.  Silver Standard, 925/1000.

| Ratio. | Gold at 77s. 9d. per oz. Standard Bank or Mint buying price. | Gold at 77s. 10½d. per oz. Standard, Mint Coining price and Bank selling price. |
|---|---|---|
|  | d. | d. |
| 15½ to 1 | 60·740 per oz. std. | 60 838 per oz. std. |
| 16 ,, 1 | 58·842 ,, | 58·936 ,, |
| 17 ,, 1 | 55·380 ,, | 55·470 ,, |
| 18 ,, 1 | 52·304 ,, | 52·389 ,, |
| 19 ,, 1 | 49·551 ,, | 49·631 ,, |
| 20 ,, 1 | 47·074 ,, | 47·149 ,, |
| 21 ,, 1 | 44·832 ,, | 44·904 ,, |

OUT-TURN OF BAR SILVER IN INDIA.

| Price in London per oz. standard. | Price per Rupee in India. | Ratio about. |
|---|---|---|
| d. | s. d. |  |
| 44 | 1 4·883 | 21½ to 1 |
| 45 | 1 5·266 | 21 ,, 1 |
| 46 | 1 5·650 |  |
| 47 | 1 6·034 | 20 ,, 1 |
| 48 | 1 6·417 |  |
| 49 | 1 6·800 | 19 ,, 1 |
| 50 | 1 7·183 |  |
| 51 | 1 7·566 |  |
| 52 | 1 7·949 | 18 ,, 1 |

SAMUEL MONTAGU.

THE

# INDIAN CURRENCY DANGER.

A Criticism of the Proposed Alterations

in the

Indian Standard.

BY

HERMANN SCHMIDT

LONDON:

EFFINGHAM WILSON & CO., ROYAL EXCHANGE.

1893.

THE following pages reproduce in an extended form some arguments which were used in a letter to the *Times* (London, 30th August, 1892), and in an article in the *Pioneer* (Allahabad, 7th September, 1892), anent proposals to tamper with the Indian Standard. These pages are published at the request of friends who desire, at a critical juncture, to place a larger public in the possession of the facts appertaining to the Currency Question in India before decisions of momentous consequences are finally taken

LONDON, *January*, 1893.

# THE

# INDIAN CURRENCY DANGER.

SINCE the adjournment of the Monetary Conference, the centre of interest of the Currency question has been shifted from Brussels to Washington and London. At Washington the great battle between the advocates of the repeal of the Sherman Act and the champions of the free coinage of silver will be fought out; in London the not less momentous question of the future of the Indian standard will be decided. We shall not discuss to-day the American aspect of the controversy, nor whether victory in the United States will eventually rest with those who desire the technical perfection of the English Gold standard, or with those who regard the currency as a great social factor, and aim at stability of purchasing power. It is our intention to confine ourselves to the Indian side of the question, to investigate the effects of the fall of the gold price of silver on India, and to examine how far separate treatment of the Indian exchange apart from the other Eastern exchanges is advisable and likely to be beneficial.

Everybody knows the history of the silver question during the last twenty years: the demonetisation of silver by Germany; the limitation and finally the suspension of the free coinage of silver in France and in the States of the Latin Union, and the consequent fall in the gold price of silver—a fall interrupted in 1878 by the passage of the Bland Bill, and in 1890 by that of the Sherman Bill, but on the whole continuous and unbroken. . The consequences of these events to the gold countries do not concern us to-day, the question for us is : What has been their effect on India ? On this question, as on many others, the opinions of experts differ with regard to important points, but, fortunately there is almost unanimous agreement upon one point—viz., that the results in India of the fall in the gold price of silver were *not* what the ablest authorities, among them Mr. W. Bagehot, expected them to be. The purchasing power of the rupee in India did *not* fall as silver declined in the London market, and the demand for silver for export to the East did *not* increase as its gold price fell. Silver in fact proved the better and stabler standard metal, the level of rupee prices altered but little, whilst gold appreciated and gold prices declined almost *pari passu* with silver. This is what constitutes the " perversity " of the rupee; hence most of the present troubles.

But if this position is once fully grasped, it is not difficult to get a tolerably clear idea of what has resulted in India from the fall in the gold price of silver. This fall has undoubtedly enabled India to command her standard metal on favourable terms, for if rupee prices for her produce have not actually risen, they have at least been kept from falling. India has therefore possessed a stimulus to profitable production such as has been unknown in the gold standard countries for the past two decades. All the test figures of India show steady and continuous improvement, such as the exports and imports, the shipping, the railways, the canals, excise, customs, post and telegraph. The great mass of the people of India have as undoubtedly benefited by the cheapening of silver as Europe benefited between 1853 and 1870 by the cheapening and greater production of gold. The silver obligations of the peasantry, amounting to very large totals, have been lightened, and so has the weight of taxes. Production has consequently been stimulated, and increased production has been followed by industrial development, of which the rapid growth of the cotton-mills of Bombay may be cited as an instance.

But there is another side to this pleasing picture. Whilst the "India of the Indians" has prospered and the toiling natives are breathing more freely under a diminishing burden of indebtedness, the foreign merchants have been exasperated by constantly fluctuating exchanges with the gold countries, the Anglo-Indian community has been suffering loss by the smaller amount of sterling which rupee salaries realise, and, above all, the Indian Government itself has been seriously embarrassed by the low exchange and the consequent high price which had to be paid for sterling bills. These bills must be purchased to the amount of £15,000,000 to £16,000,000 per annum in payment for different "home charges," principally interest on debt contracted in gold. Every fall of a penny in

the exchange means a " loss " to the Indian Government of about £1,000,000, and this "loss" is
progressive—*i.e.*, it increases per penny with each
fall of the exchange. This extra cost of purchasing
sterling is seriously disturbing the Indian budgets,
and circumstances might arise that would lead to
grave financial difficulties which could not fail to
re-act unfavourably on the whole population. The
Government considers it, consequently, a duty imposed by the highest political considerations to
arrest this rise in gold, and, if possible, even to
turn the current of exchange; and in this the
Government are right, provided, however, it can
be done without detriment to the commercial and
economic condition of the country.

Many able men have, of course, endeavoured to
find a remedy for the evils here sketched. For
years bi-metallism was considered in India *the*
remedy, and its advent looked forward to for salvation; but bi-metallism, to be effective, must be
adopted in conjunction with England, and England
has so far refused to move in that direction. The
fear now is that action may become necessary in
India before bi-metallism is practicable; and to
this fear we owe the different proposals which have
of late come to the front and which we purpose to
examine.

These proposals may be classed under three
different heads :

(I.) To close the Indian mints to the private
coinage of silver, with or without power to
the Government to continue coining if necessary;

(II.) To introduce a gold standard, with or without a gold currency.

(III.) To impose a higher seigniorage.

The object which all these three proposals have in view is the same—viz., to make the price of the rupee more or less independent of the value of silver, and, if possible, to raise the gold price of the rupee above its actual level. It is argued that in this way most of the evils at present so severely felt would be removed. The Indian Government would be able to buy the necessary gold on cheaper terms, the growing loss on the Council bills would be reduced, Indian trade would no longer be disturbed by fluctuating and declining exchanges, Indian banks would see their sterling capital, placed in India, protected against further depreciation and perhaps return to something like its former value ; English holders of rupee paper would be saved from further losses on their investment ; and last, but not least, Anglo-Indial officials would be able to purchase more sterling with their rupee salaries.

It is true that Bentham,* no mean authority, declared the forced elevation of the value of money to be " fraudulent bankruptcy " and a " foolish fraud," but where the advantages seem so manifold and self-evident as in this case, it would be idle to expect that we could dispose of the matter by a reference to an authority, and we shall have to prove in detail how the proposals would be likely to work, and why they would fail to accomplish their purpose.

* " Principles of the Civil Code."

# CLOSING THE MINTS.

The first remedy suggested is the stoppage of the private coinage of silver in India. We will explain what this means. At present India possesses an automatic metallic standard, based upon Silver. Technically it is a perfect standard, as perfect as is the gold standard of England. India is, indeed, one of the very few countries of the world which still possess a perfect automatic standard. The Indian, like the English, standard coins will undergo successfully the ordeal of fire. If you melt the Indian coins down, the metal obtained will be worth as much as were the coins, a small charge for seigniorage excepted. This state of things it is proposed to alter. The further production of rupees is to be prohibited—in any case on private account—and the rupees already existing are to be invested with a monopoly value. The Government would sell its Council bills in London at this fixed value only, and as bar silver could then no longer compete with the Council bills, it is argued that people requiring drafts upon India would have to pay the Council rate, which by this means would be successfully maintained. India would then possess what has been termed a " gold standard without gold," but what in reality would be an inconvertible monopoly standard. What such a scheme means to the commerce and industry of the country can be best realised if we think that the right to convert gold into sovereigns be taken away in England without any other metal being admitted to the privilege of coinage, and with further "sterling" only obtainable by purchasing bills or transfers on London from a Government office in India. Englishmen would not stand such a system for twenty-four hours, and yet this is what is seriously proposed by able people for the benefit of the Indians.

Without, however, going further into either the legal or moral aspect of this question, we will at once proceed to sketch the position of the Indian standard after the proposed step is taken. The Indian circulation would still be silver, but silver unable to undergo the ordeal of fire. The value of the coins would be different from the value of the silver they contain. The money of India would be credit money, possessing all the attributes of inconvertible paper—it would be a standard of "metallic assignats." This credit money, however, unlike any other credit money, we are told will remain steady in its relation to gold—in fact stability in relation to gold is the chief benefit to be conferred by the adoption of this proposal. We submit that this is an extraordinary delusion.

The two means by which it is expected to fix the value of the new Indian credit money are limitation of issue and decreeing an official parity to gold. If, however, by these means paper could be fixed in its relation to gold, some at least of the numerous countries which have suffered or are suffering from the evils of fluctuating paper money would surely have remedied these evils long ago by adopting that course. Some indeed have tried it, but none have succeeded. The fact is, it cannot be done.

But we are told that India is in a position different from all other countries because, firstly, there are the weekly Council bills, and, secondly, there is a large favourable balance of trade.

Further consideration will show that this supposed exceptional position of India is a myth.

The Council bills are the drafts on India which the Government has to sell in order to provide for the " home charges " already mentioned—*i.e.*, in order to pay for interest on debt and on guaranteed railways, for stores, for army pensions, administration, &c. Sometimes this is called the " tribute " of India, a misleading expression, for tribute is an acknowledgment of submission, whilst these charges are for value and consideration received, the only question that may be debated being whether value and consideration are in all cases equal to the cost. We lay particular stress on these facts, because nothing has contributed more to obscure this subject than the idea which has widely obtained that the Council bills, in their nature or effect, are something different from other commercial bills on India, of which millions are drawn every year.* This is not so. Of course, if we could abolish the Council bills, the exchanges would move in favour of India, but they would do so still more if Lancashire were to supply India with her goods *gratis*, and refrained from drawing against them.

Even some single merchant houses have very large amounts to draw, which of late years have increased owing to greater trade. And yet Mr. H. D. Macleod maintains that the Council bills, which for twelve years have hardly increased, are mainly responsible for the fall of the gold price of silver!

The Council bills, therefore, are evidence of indebtedness. India is, "capitalistically" considered, a debtor country, like, for instance Argentina or Brazil. If Argentina or Brazil, instead of remitting to England the moneys for coupons or other Government liabilities, would establish an agency in London and every week sell bills or transfers on Buenos Ayres or Rio de Janeiro, their case and India's would be almost analogous. But no one would dream of suggesting this method for preventing the fluctuations of the gold premium at Buenos Ayres or for restoring the exchange at Rio. If the Council bills were really an instrument with which one could control the Exchanges, it follows that this power of control must grow in proportion to the total of the bills, and we should come to the *reductio ad absurdum* that the larger India's indebtedness the greater the power of the Government over the Exchanges. We repeat, therefore, the Council bills differ in no way in their effect from other bills, the only advantage arising out of the fact that one drawer has such important amounts to sell, consists in a better market-control, and even that lasts only as long as the Council can afford to hold out, and provided there are numerous and eager buyers. This last circumstance depends upon the balance of trade.

With this diagnosis of the nature and effect of the Council bills before us, we can judge ourselves of the soundness or otherwise of many of the proposals for an improvement in the Indian Currency. Difficult as it seems to believe, scarcely a week passes without some brand-new theory being started in the newspapers, the gist of which consists in controlling the Indian Exchange by means of the Council Bills. What is, and in its very nature must remain a factor of weakness in the situation — indebtedness — is over and over again mistaken by superficial thinkers for a strong point, and actually proposed as a means of defence. Confusion of ideas and want of knowledge could not go further.

We will now examine the second factor, in which those who think India exceptionally situated place their trust—the favourable balance of the trade of India. We are afraid we shall find this equally unreliable. India occupies by no means an unique position with regard to her balance of trade. Other countries have a favourable balance, yet some of those have been unable to maintain their currency stable in its relation to gold—for instance, Argentina and Brazil. All debtor countries must have a favourable trade-balance if they are to remain solvent. A great part of the Indian balance is required to pay for freight as well as for interest and dividends on foreign capital, in addition to the liabilities on Council bills. But India's favourable trade-balance is no Heaven-ordained eternal law of nature. Although of long standing it depends upon certain conditions, and nothing more disastrous to, and destructive of, these conditions could be imagined than the proposal to close the Indian mints to the private coinage of silver.

Let us explain. The price of silver depends upon demand and supply. The principal demand for the precious metals — that demand which determines their price — is the Mint Demand.

Because since 1873 silver has ceased to be coined into money by a great number of States, that have taken to gold instead, the gold price of silver has fallen. To-day there are only two great countries left which continue largely to absorb silver for currency purposes—the United States and India: the former by purchases, the latter by open mints. If these mints are now to be closed to private parties, one of the two remaining supports to silver will be taken away and the gold price of silver will fall immediately and severely. The opinion has been expressed that, some time after such a measure is taken, silver would improve again, but for that opinion there is no ground whatever. Even if many of the mines should discontinue working, there can be no rise in the price of silver, because there will not be sufficient demand. Of course the American demand will still exist* ; but even assuming Legislation in the United States to continue unaltered, that demand alone will not suffice to help silver to recovery. But this fall in the gold price of silver will have a great effect on the Indian trade.

India is in a very different position from all other countries which, so far, have discarded silver. She is surrounded by silver - using nations. China, Japan, the Straits, and Persia, have the silver standard, and are likely for a long time to come to continue to use it. Now,

---

* Should India close her mints, it will be easy for the United States to continue the Sherman Act. Purchases being stipulated in ounces, their value will become less and less as silver falls further. A repeal will hardly be required, the Sherman Act would then repeal itself.

while the closing of the Indian Mints and the fixing of a gold value to the rupee would, at least for a time, steady the gold exchanges in India, those very measures would disturb the hitherto steady silver exchanges in an unprecedented manner. The Indian exports to "the further East," which at present amount to Rx. 25,000,000 per annum, and which show a balance in favour of India of Rx. 15,000,000 per annum (of which Rx. 2,000,000 are settled by imports of silver, and the rest mostly through London by sterling bills), would at once be disorganised, perhaps become impossible. This alone might suffice to upset the present favourable Indian trade balance, which, after making the necessary allowances, amounts to hardly £8,000,000.* But this is not all. Such a divergence of the Indian from the remaining silver exchanges would greatly hamper the producers of India in the sale and export of their produce. With such articles as tea, opium, silk, indigo, seeds, sugar, the Indians would at once acutely feel the competition of China, Japan, and the Straits in the markets of the world, and India might with regard to some or all of them find that she was beaten and supplanted. In fact those countries "further East" would then occupy towards India the very position which India holds

* The average excess of merchandise exports over imports for the last five years are Rx. 32,000,000, or, deducting Council bills, Rx. 12,000,000, or £7,500,000. All amounts for hoarding, wear and tear, freight, and interest on private investments, &c., must be deducted therefrom. It is evident from these figures that the imports of silver into India (which amount to over Rx. 12,000,000 per annum) partly represent fresh capital sent out.

to-day towards Europe, and to which she is indebted for so many advantages. Their production, their commerce, their exports would grow and expand, whilst India would be strangled by the rope which a restricted standard with a fixed gold value* would throw around her. Of course a fall of prices within India, corresponding to and counterbalancing the further decline of silver outside India would remedy this position, but experts declare that Indian prices cannot decline considerably without affecting production, and through production, exports. In one way or another, therefore, the exports of India would suffer : if Indian prices keep up, they would suffer owing to the competition of the remaining silver countries ; and similarly if Indian prices fall, owing to declining production within India. But the Council bills must be sold in London as each Wednesday comes round, unless the dangerous and in the long run impossible expedient of a large and continuous increase of the gold debt of India be resorted to. Sooner or later the point will be reached when the Council bills on offer exceed the demand for remittances to the East, as on the Council alone would fall the whole brunt of keeping up the Exchange, because everybody else would sell his exchange a fraction below the Council rate to make sure of his " sterling." But on that Wednesday when it became known in the

* This gold value would be fixed by the Government at the exchange ruling at the time when the Mints were closed, if not indeed at a higher exchange. It has been explained above how this rate would be much higher than the parity of silver the very day after the Mints are closed.

City that the Council were unable to dispose of their drafts, India's artificial monopoly standard of "metallic assignats" would collapse, and a calamity would ensue of dimensions impossible to estimate.*

In the above exposition we have assumed that silver has entirely ceased to be coined. Should, however, the Government retain the right to coin for their own account, and exercise such right, the result would be increased difficulty to maintain exchange (for the silver will have to be purchased by gold), and the collapse of the new standard would come all the quicker.

As a proof that exchange does affect India's balance of trade we shall quote the figures for the merchandise exports and imports for the last two completed financial years :—

|  | 1891-92. | 1890-91. |
|---|---|---|
| Exports ... | ...Rx. 108,036,000 | Rx. 100,185,700 |
| Imports ... ... | 66,587,500 | 69,034,900 |
| Difference | ...Rx. 41,448,500 | Rx. 31,100,800 |

We quite admit that these figures are not by themselves absolute proof, as a great deal depends upon the harvest; but in this case the harvest has not been a special factor, a shortage of cotton in 1891-92 being counterbalanced by abundant wheat. Moreover, Mr. J. E. O'Conor says in reference thereto : "Thus the excess of exports, which was abnormally small in 1890-91,

* This is no argument against a rise of exchange owing to an improvement in the gold price of silver. Such a rise would happen simultaneously in all silver countries and not handicap India against the further East.

was as abnormally large in 1891–92, both the results following the fluctuations of exchange, which affected trade in a contrary sense in each of the two years." And if this happened while the trade of the other silver countries was under the same influences as that of India, what would happen if the other countries were to compete with India on unprecedentedly favourable terms?

We have sketched the manner in which a monopoly standard would work, and how it would come to grief. In doing so we had to admit that for a time the situation would be relieved—viz., till the Government had to deal with the problem of an adverse balance of trade, so much more difficult than the problem of an adverse exchange. As we cannot and do not pretend to be able to fix the time when the trade balance would turn, there might be opportunists quite willing to accept the immediate improvement, which is not denied, and to leave the future to avert the threatened collapse which, it could be argued, might never come. For those we will lift the veil from the "improvement" which exchange brings about, so that they may recognise that there is nothing mysterious about it. The idea of righting things by "exchange" and producing satisfactory results without apparently any cost to anybody, is so fascinating that it will do good to show that here, as everywhere else in political economy, somebody pays for the advantages obtained. If the Government and their servants benefit by the monopoly standard—as long as it works—the reason is that a virtual increase of taxation takes place if the rupee is fixed at an artificially high gold value.

B

Instead of having to go to the trouble of finding and levying fresh taxes, the officials attain the same object by altering the value of the money in which the taxes are due, retaining old names but giving them new meanings. The Government, in fact, gets rid of the currency difficulty by transferring the loss to the people of India. Whether this is just is not now the question. All we desire to point out is that if it be possible to collect virtually higher taxes after the mints are closed— *i.e.*, when conditions generally are certain to be less favourable than to-day—it must be possible to increase the taxes to-day; if, however, as is sometimes alleged, the latter is impracticable, it follows that under the monopoly standard the taxes would not come in. The result would be that instead of shifting the burden of the exchange loss unto the people, the Government would have then to face the problem of diminishing revenue, instead of, as to-day, that of dear gold.

But while the advantages to the Government are all problematical, there is the certainty of a loss which would be suffered through the opium revenue. The Indian opium constitutes a Government monopoly, and is exported to China. There is no question that a part, if not the whole, of the loss resulting from the difference which would then exist between the Indian and the Chinese standard, would have to be borne by the Indian Government, and there would be thus a serious set-off against the savings on " exchange."

Before leaving this part of our subject, there remain two points which ought to be mentioned. The first is the danger of illicit coinage of the monopoly rupee. This danger exists, but we do not attach much importance to it. Experience has shown that practically it may be ignored if proper supervision is exercised.

Much more importance attaches to the second point—viz., the loss which would be suffered by the natives from the depreciation of the untold quantities of uncoined silver in their possession. These hoards constitute to a large extent the savings of the natives, who for generations have looked upon them as synonymous with money. By a stroke of the pen of an "alien" Government, whose object would be misunderstood, these masses of silver would be reduced to a mere fraction of their previous value, and here may be the germ of grave political difficulties. From one end of India to the other the cry will be—" The Sircar has taken our wealth away." The recklessness of statesmen who would be willing to run such risks, and to create this dissatisfaction in order to gain ephemeral and problematical advantages, would be unpardonable.

We therefore find that the closing of the Indian mints to the private coinage of silver and the introduction of an inconvertible monopoly standard would be a dangerous makeshift, which it would be impossible to maintain permanently, and which would ultimately lead to endless difficulties and confusion.

## A GOLD STANDARD.

We will now examine the second proposal—viz., to establish a gold standard in India. As a great many of our arguments with regard to this case will be on the same lines as those already made use of, we shall not repeat them in detail, and shall therefore be able to treat this part of our subject in less space.

As long as thirty years ago a gold standard was strongly advocated for India. But this was done for precisely the opposite reasons which are given to-day. At that time silver was scarce, "dear," and appreciating, and the idea was to substitute gold for silver as the standard metal for India, so as to let that country participate in the progress which was then perceptible in Europe, owing to a plentiful supply of currency. To-day it is the "cheapness" of silver which has suggested the transition from silver to gold.

The gold standard is, of course, not open to the objections raised against the monopoly rupee on account of the latter being unable to undergo the ordeal of fire. A real gold standard is as automatic and as perfect as the present silver standard of India. But, unfortunately, this real gold standard is what nobody thinks of introducing into India. It could only be established by accumulating sufficient gold to replace the greater part of the silver at present in circulation in India, reducing the remaining silver money to token coinage, and making gold (or notes based on gold) sole legal tender. But everybody is agreed that this is out of question, for it would be as impossible to sell the silver as to find the necessary gold.

The gold standard which is proposed for India is of an inferior kind. The schemes differ in

detail, but more or less they all agree with that of
the Indian Currency Association, which may be
taken as typical. The aim is to establish a kind
of *limping standard* after the pattern exhibited by
France and Holland.* Gold is to be made legal
tender, maintaining also as legal tender the existing rupees, while stopping their further coinage.†
The point, however, which the Indian Currency
Association overlooks is that, in order to make
this policy a success, it must also be preceded by
the accumulation of a large quantity of gold,
sufficient to maintain a parity between gold and
the old silver money. If the gold be insufficient
India would not get the standard of France, but
lapse into the monetary condition of Spain, where

* How unfavourably Continental authorities judge of such
a state of things may be gathered from the following remarks
of Mr. O. Haupt regarding Holland :—"Apart from all other
considerations the Dutch money, like all good and honest
money, should in itself possess that value which belongs to it
by comparison with foreign money of the same kind and
quality. . . . . This is a question which rests solely on
economic laws, which are well defined and rule the whole
world, except where the vision is clouded by the monetary
confusion, which seems, at least in some countries, the cha-
racteristic sign of our times." — *Histoire monétaire de notre
temps.*

† There is sometimes an idea that even under such a
scheme the Government may be allowed to continue coining
silver, but this is an absurdity. As it is it will be exceedingly
difficult to maintain the rupees at " par," but if fresh rupees
were coined this would be impossible. In Holland the Government is so much alive to this danger that when fresh
token money is required it does not buy ingots, but melts
down florins, though the other course would give a large
profit.

the system is the same as in France, but where the Government has coined silver to excess, so that the currency is depreciated, and gold at a premium. This is a serious danger, for it would be almost criminal folly to deprive India of her automatic silver standard in order to plunge her into the vortex of a nondescript depreciated inconvertible currency, fluctuating daily and probably severely in its relation to gold.

The practical question is how much gold would India require to safely start the limping standard. We shall not attempt to answer this question absolutely, but certain figures exist to guide us. France finds £160,000,000 gold sufficient to keep £130,000,000 silver "at par," Holland is able to maintain the parity with £8,000,000 gold (or gold bills) against £11,000,000 silver, while Spain finds £8,000,000 gold insufficient to maintain at par £25,000,000 silver. One gold to three silver seems therefore the minimum proportion. The Indian rupees are estimated at £150,000,000; if European conditions afford any guidance, there will be thus at least £50,000,000 of gold required for India. Where and how to obtain this sum we should like to be told by the Indian Currency Association.

But after this gold has been secured it has to be retained, and here will be the real difficulty. For the introduction of the gold standard into India will be accompanied or followed by most of the economic disturbances depicted when we treated of the effects of the monopoly rupee. Exports and imports will be interfered with, producers and manufacturers will be handicapped, the revenue will suffer from the decline of the railway and canal traffics and the falling off in the opium returns. Meanwhile the people of India would suffer from the evils under which England is groaning, the well-recognised evils of an appreciating standard. In the end the balance of trade will become unfavourable. Then will come the question how to retain the gold in the country, and this difficulty no writer has so far attempted to face. All we are told is that English capital would flow into the country and keep everything straight, but this is a great mistake. English capital has gone and is still going to India in spite of the exchanges, because of the prospects of large profits. English capital will cease to go, even should exchanges be guaranteed against fluctuations, after the opportunities for profitable employment have vanished. Indeed, the very fact that India is, capitalistically speaking, a debtor country will render the maintenance of the gold standard a very difficult and very delicate matter, for foreign capital can be called back from India at any time, and the very act of converting capital which now represents silver into gold may make many people desirous of taking it away as long as gold can be had for it. The return flow of rupee paper from England to India may alone suffice to upset the exchanges. We therefore say deliberately the gold of India, if ever successfully accumulated, would be exported, and monetary difficulties of the gravest kind would follow. There would then be a premium on gold, and great fluctuations in exchanges, creating a situation worse than any so far experienced.

This consummation would be reached all the sooner should the advice given in some quarters be accepted, and a " gold standard without a gold currency " be introduced ; for, as is evident, the gold reserves would then be much smaller, and consequently more quickly exhausted.

Some think that the Indian Government being in good credit, its promise to pay in gold would be sufficient to prevent a fall of the exchange below " par " ; but in monetary matters Government promises count for nothing, performance is everything. The merchant who requires gold for export does not want the credit or bond of the Indian administration, and if he cannot get the gold, a premium will be the result.

We therefore find that the same forces which would upset the monopoly standard, would also kill the gold standard, unless the country would be prepared to make sacrifices which are out of all proportion to the advantages in view. As to the evils from which the Indian Government suffers, they would not be removed by the adoption of either of these proposals ; and this is easily explained. for these evils exist outside of India, and cannot therefore be cured by reforms within India. These evils have one common origin : the appreciation of gold. India has contracted gold liabilities. She has to discharge these liabilities in produce, and on the gold price of this produce depends the quantity she has to export.*

* In his speech at Calcutta on 13th July, 1892, Mr. James Mackay, President of the Indian Currency Association, said : " The granaries of India will not become African deserts, nor will the flavour of China tea be preferred to that of Indian,

Whether within her own confines that gold price remains gold or is converted into silver or copper, or any other material, does not alter in any way the burden of these gold liabilities. India shares in this respect the fate of all other countries with a foreign gold debt. The weight of debt has increased for her, but only as much as it has for others. She has to export more wheat, more cotton, &c., to discharge the same amount of gold liability; but so has, for instance, Australia in spite of her gold standard. The only difference is that in India the change is visible through the fall of the exchange, whilst in Australia it is hidden by the general fall in prices; that in India the loss falls direct on the Government, whilst in Australia it falls first on the people, and on the Government only indirectly. The result is the same in both instances. Australia receives less gold for her produce. India receives about the former number of rupees, but loses in converting these rupees into sterling. Whatever India loses to-day is therefore not caused by any fault inherent in silver or the rupee, but by general conditions affecting the whole world, and caused by the appreciation of gold. Any alteration of the *status* of the rupee does not alter the general conditions, and cannot, therefore, be a remedy. This explains why India can do nothing to cure the evil, and why all those schemes which at present apparently

though we insist on our produce being paid for in gold." Does Mr. Mackay maintain that the exports of India are at present paid for in anything else than gold ? Does not India settle by them gold liabilities ? The error is extraordinary and significant !

exercise great fascination over some people, only amount to a hidden, surreptitious, and, in our opinion temporary, shifting of the incidence of the evils.

But though India can do nothing to remove the evils, she may do a good deal to augment them, and she would do so if she adopted gold as a standard. If the Indian currency demands were to come on the market, and increase still more the inquiry for gold, there would be a further fall in gold prices, and the burden of India's gold liabilities would be still further enhanced. But it will not only be India's *currency* demands which will be in gold, her *hoarding* demands would be for gold also. Some writers have given expression to the extraordinary idea that after the opening of the Indian Mints to the coinage of gold, the hoarded gold will be coined and get into circulation. Quite the reverse will happen. The natives who now hoard principally silver will find this metal no longer a desirable treasure, and will in future hoard nothing but gold. Viewed in the light of these last considerations, we must confess that the proposal of introducing a gold standard into India would in all probability prove even more disastrous to India than the proposed monopoly standard, though on technical grounds the former is preferable to the latter.

There are, however, we admit, two classes of people that would considerably gain by an alteration of the Indian standard in either of the two ways proposed. The first class are the Anglo-Indian officials. Whether this is a case for special consideration is a subject outside the scope of these pages. It is clear, however, that, should India's prosperity decline, a number of these officials would become superfluous, so with some, at least, it is not a question whether to receive sterling or rupees, but whether rupees or nothing. But, after all, this is a class interest, and surely nobody would recommend legislation for the purpose of serving it. The same must be said of the other set of people who would benefit by a change of standard, the European holders of rupee paper. They have taken an investment exposed to all the risks of silver. That this investment has turned out unfortunate may entitle them to our sympathy, but would not justify legislative interference.

But we are told that the monetary system or systems which, in the course of the foregoing examination, we found ought to be condemned have been introduced into other countries, and have worked there satisfactorily. In reply to this we have to repeat what we stated before—that the position of India is in many respects peculiar, and that it is quite possible for a system which answers in a capitalistic country like, say, Holland, to prove a disastrous failure in capital-owing India. Nor would the experience of some small country be any guide to the effects likely to follow in India. In finance the Latin " *quod licet Jovi, non licet bovi* " has often to be reversed. But in our opinion these reservations are not even necessary with regard to the cases quoted as precedents for India, because an examination will show that they are in no sense parallel cases.

The most frequently-quoted " example " is Java. That country resembles India in many respects, but it discontinued the coinage of silver in 1875, the mint being in Holland, and later adopted gold as a standard. However, very little gold is used in Java, the circulation is silver, and even the bank reserves consist principally of silver. Nevertheless, Java is no precedent for India. For the silver money of Java is identical with the silver money which is unlimited legal tender in Holland, and Java's currency is thus guaranteed and kept "at par" by the Dutch gold reserves. If the Java exchange turns "unfavourable" the Java silver is exported to Amsterdam, and, if necessary, gold is procured there with it. To establish a basis for comparison between India and Java, we should have to admit rupees into England as full legal tender. But the economic events in Java subsequent to the introduction of the gold standard are instructive, as they go far to confirm what was stated above about the consequences likely to happen in India. Beginning with the year 1875, there has been an extraordinary change for the worse in the economic and financial condition of Java. Up to that year that colony enjoyed continuous surpluses, amounting since 1831 to a total of about 800 million florins (which the Dutchmen used in order to balance their own budgets); but with 1876 there began a series of years of deficits, necessitating loans from the Dutch Government, which amounted in 1883 to 45 million florins, but which have since been mostly repaid. In the movement of merchandise there was after 1875 a tendency towards decrease in the exports, and towards increase in the imports, and the bullion movements on private account, which used to show a balance of imports, showed betwen 1875 and 1883 large balances of exports. It is only fair to state that undoubtedly other causes contributed to bring about these unfavourable results, as just at that period the crops were much damaged ; but it is at least a remarkable " coincidence " that in Java the very events which economic reasonings predicted would happen from a change of standard, actually did happen. In his very able and exhaustive treatise of this subject, Mr. Van den Berg, a rather unwilling witness—for his influence had been largely instrumental in carrying the change of standard—had to confess that this change had caused injury to a section of the community, whilst in India things had taken quite another turn from what he anticipated.

No more to the point than Java as a precedent for India is the other country often referred to in this connection — viz., Austria. That country suspended in 1879 the right of private coinage for silver. But the step only meant the adhesion to the *régime* of paper money. There was no " fixed par " either with gold or silver, and no pretence of such ; and the gold exchanges fluctuated daily, as they do in other paper-money countries. These fluctuations were sometimes considerable, but on the whole not excessive, as times were peaceful and the country was prospering. If India likes to try this experiment, let her do so openly, but it will not be a " gold standard," not even a " gold standard without gold." India, however, is surrounded by silver countries, which Austria was not, and her experience would, we contend, be very different from that of Austria. Her financial

secretary would have to undertake a new duty—
viz., that of watching and guarding exchange,
which is no mere sinecure and might force him to
become as expert in *operations de bourse* as his
colleague at St. Petersburg. Only within the last
few months has Austria decided to formally adopt
a gold standard, and in order to introduce the
same she is preparing to do what we said that
India would have to do under similar circumstances—viz., to accumulate a sufficient stock of
gold, for which purpose Austria is endeavouring to
raise a foreign loan.

Paper was also virtually the standard in another
instance, which is sometimes given as a precedent
for India—viz., in Holland, between 1873 and
1875, i.e., after her mints were closed to silver,
and before they were opened to gold. Holland
being a capitalistic and creditor country, and
possessing at that time a favourable trade balance,
her paper money became appreciated, and gold
was introduced to put a stop to this appreciation.

We thus find that there is no virtue in the
so-called historical precedents for the monetary systems, whose introduction into India we
deprecate.

Before we proceed further, we think it advisable
to examine specifically some of the definite schemes
which have lately been discussed, and which aim
at removing the Indian exchange difficulty by the
introduction of some kind of a gold standard.

The worst proposals in this direcion undoubtedly emanate from that class of counsellors
who may be termed "cambiomaniacs"—i.e., from
people who only look to exchange, and to

nothing but exchange. For them a country with an exchange "at par" is a prosperous country, and the most prosperous country of all is England on account of her technically perfect gold standard. They do not trouble whether gold appreciates, nor whether economic disturbances arise from such appreciation; their happiness is assured by "gold parity." This happiness they desire to confer upon India. There may be a doubt in their minds whether 1s. 10⅝d. or 2s. is the "correct" par, but they are generally accommodating and willing to take either. "Perish India, as long as exchange is re-established," is their motto. As an example of this order of thought we recommend the perusal of a little French pamphlet, "L'Étalon d'Or aux Indes et la Roupie au pair."

There is no recent English proposal of equal boldness. Fixity of exchange in the neighbourhood of the actual quotations is the object generally aimed at. The proposal which of late has come most to the front is that made by the Indian Currency Association, which relies simply on closed mints and the free play of the foreign exchanges of India not only to retain gold but actually to supply that country with the gold necessary for her standard. How unjustifiable we consider such reliance to be, we need not tell our readers after the exposition we have given in these pages. It is no answer to say, as Mr. Mackay does, that if the Indian trade balance under the gold standard were to turn against India, she would then be in no worse position than if the same happened in the present day; for we have shown that the introduction of the gold standard would be the very cause of the unfavourable change in the trade balance.

The same criticism applies to Mr. William Douglas' proposals in " The Currency of India." Indeed, as far as we can judge, the method suggested by the Indian Currency Association is very much on the lines of those proposals. Mr. Douglas thinks he makes a great point in showing that it is not the Indian *exchange*, but the *standard* itself, that has fallen ; but his figures only prove that, all through the fall in silver, exchange has kept favourable for India, necessitating the import of silver to settle the account. This, however, is only another way of stating that the balance of trade was favourable. After the introduction of the gold standard this would cease to be the case, and, to speak Mr. Douglas' language, we should then have a " rise in the standard," and a " fall in the exchange." Where would India's gold be then ?

A proposal which has been several times referred to in the London Press is contained in " Ricardo's Exchange Remedy," by A. M. L., known to be Mr. A. M. Lindsay, of the Bank of Bengal. This remedy consists, besides closing the mints and artificially rating the rupee, in setting aside £5,000,000 of the Bank of England reserve to be devoted to the purchase and re-sale of silver for the benefit of India. We fail to see the connection between this scheme and the name of Ricardo, who never countenanced any other value for standard money than its value as bullion. But apart from that, the conversion of £5,000,000 sterling of our gold reserves into silver—and this apparently without consideration being given—seems inadvisable, as these reserves, according to the highest authority, are already insufficient. Moreover, £5,000,000 sterling is ridiculously inadequate for the purpose of guaranteeing the whole circulation of India. Mr. Lindsay's proposals consequently have not found many supporters, although he shows great knowledge in his treatment of the details of the subject.

The latest scheme before the public is that of Mr. L. C. Probyn.* He wishes to introduce the gold standard by creating an unit of R. 10,000 and making at first only notes of that amount convertible into gold. In this way he hopes to attract and to retain gold, but the result of his scheme would only be that all the notes below R. 10,000 and all the silver rupees would fall to a discount and the currency of India be totally disorganised.

As we remarked above, the object of the English proposals has of late been not so much to rehabilitate the rupee by raising it to its old value as to prevent it from falling lower. The contention, of course, is that up to the present time the fall of the rupee, however inconvenient, was bearable, but that the limit has now been reached, beyond which things cannot be allowed to drift. We must admit that such a limit exists, but it is not a hard and fast one ; for, given time, it will be possible for the Indian situation to gradually accommodate itself to lower exchanges, probably to any exchange that may be quoted as long as

* *Journal of the Institute of Bankers*, January, 1893.

America continues her purchases of silver. The great difficulty will be for the Government to balance its budget while exchange keeps falling. But, though this difficulty is considerable, it may be, and we think it has been, exaggerated. A great part of the loss on exchange, as shown by the accounts, is owing to the method of book-keeping; but, without making any allowance whatever for this circumstance, the following figures prove that exchange is not the only item of Government expenditure that has increased.

|  | 1879–80 | 1892–93 (Budget Estimate.) |
|---|---|---|
| Total Expenditure ... | Rx. 60,948,000 | Rx. 88,221,300 |
| Loss by Exchange ... | „ 3,246,000 | „ 7,975,200 |
|  | Rx. 57,697,000 | Rx. 80,246,100 |
|  |  | „ 57,697,000 |
| Increase outside Exchange... |  | Rx. 22,549,100 |

It seems difficult to believe that the Indian Government, which never says anything about the 22 crores of additional general expenditure, should come to grief over a crore or two further loss on exchange. Moreover, some compensation for the heavier weight of the gold debt must come to the Government from their 900 millions of rupees of silver debt. As a matter of fact we find that with the exchange at about 1s. 4d. the Indian budget has shown a surplus, whilst deficits have occurred with a much higher exchange. We look upon the present position with all the less alarm when we find that already in January, 1886, exchange being then over 1s. 6d., an official despatch stated:—" We are drifting into a position of the most serious financial embarrassment, in regard to the consequences of which, not only as regards our financial position, but in respect of measures of taxation in relation to our rule in British India, it is impossible not to be seriously apprehensive."

The position of the Indian Government is therefore perhaps less endangered than is sometimes supposed. As long as the rupee shows no indication of becoming depreciated * in India, even the Indian Government ought to be able to master the situation.

## A HIGHER SEIGNIORAGE.

We now come to the consideration of the last of the three proposals for improving the Indian currency—viz., the imposition of a higher seigniorage. A seigniorage is a charge made by the authorities for converting the money metal into standard coins. In India this charge is at present 2 per cent. In a speech at the London Chamber of Commerce (26th October, 1892), Sir John Lubbock suggested a seigniorage of 10 per cent.,

---

* Mr. A. S. HARVEY, in his speech at the Institute of Bankers (see *Journal,* January, 1893), stated that it is impossible to maintain that the best standard for any nation is that which is depreciating most rapidly in comparison with the standard of the country with which it deals. We fail to see this impossibility as regards India, as long as that depreciation is only *relative.* Of course we should put the case differently, and say that that standard is the best for any nation which remains steady, whilst that of the country with which it deals is appreciating.

and others, before and after him, have proposed a similar course.

At first sight these suggestions look attractive, and we will at once admit that the evils resulting from adopting such a policy will be small in comparison to the evils resulting from closing the mints or adopting the gold standard. But then, on the other hand, the advantages from this policy will also be small. Moreover, by following this course we should not get a stable exchange, which is promised to us, though, we contend, erroneously, by the two policies previously considered. With the seigniorage of 10 per cent., exchange would keep 10 per cent. above the parity of silver; but at that distance it would follow the fluctuations of silver from day to day. The probability, indeed, is that the adoption of this seigniorage would at once reduce the price of bar silver in the London market, so that exchange itself would hardly alter. As to the economic result it would handicap the exports of India in comparison to the exports of other silver countries to the extent of the additional 8 per cent. seigniorage—in other words, it would be equal to an *export duty of 8 per cent.* It is quite possible that the Indian trade could well afford to pay this duty, but in that case we think it better for the Government to impose this duty direct, instead of only levying it in the form of an extra seigniorage.

But while the question of a fixed seigniorage is relatively a small matter, the most decided objection should be raised against another kind of seigniorage proposed — viz. a varying charge equal to any fall which may take place in silver below a fixed price. Sometimes this proposal takes the form of charging an import duty of that kind on silver. We will say nothing about the practical difficulty of fixing a daily varying duty, and the endless confusion which would ensue. It will suffice to state that this proposal would have the same economic results and affect exchange and commerce in precisely the same way as the closing of the mints, and would eventually produce the same collapse. In fact this collapse would probably come sooner, as it would still be possible to convert silver into money.

We have completed our survey. We find that all the schemes proposed—the monopoly standard, the gold standard, the seigniorage—resolve themselves ultimately into disguised taxation. Yet these schemes have been suggested with the very object of avoiding further taxation. Surely under these circumstances it is better statesmanship to act openly than by stealth. The Indian Currency Danger consists in the latter course being adopted, *i.e.*, in taxation being imposed by tampering with the standard, which would affect the relations of millions of people and possibly destroy the trade of an Empire.

The Indian authorities have so far refused to take the leap in the dark which a change in the Indian standard implies. There is every reason to believe that further investigation of this question will only lead to more resolute adherence to the policy hitherto pursued, under which in trying and difficult times Indian commerce has flourished and Indian wealth has increased.

EFFINGHAM WILSON & Co., Printers, Royal Exchange, London, E.C.

# CLOSING OF THE INDIAN MINTS.

It may be conceded that, in view of the condition of Indian finance and the violent disturbances to trade consequent upon the fluctuations and fall in the gold price of silver, the Government were fully justified in doing something; but it was not necessary for them to do the wrong thing.

Ever since 1873 the relation between the gold money of England and the silver money of India has been subject to a series of dislocations. In other words, the relative value of the sovereign and the rupee has been seriously disturbed. More than this: Owing to the enormous fall in the gold price of silver, the rupee, which used to be worth from 1s. 10d. to 2s. in English money, has gradually declined in value, till it lately became worth only 1s. 2½d.

The consequence has been that the finances of India and the trade between England and India have both, for the last twenty years, been thrown out of gear. Many new conditions have arisen, some tending in one direction, some in another, but all abnormal and unsettling. So far back as 1876, when the gold equivalent of the rupee had fallen to nearly 1s. 6d., the Indian Government took the matter into their serious consideration. But a slight, and, as it turned out, a temporary recovery at the end of that year, relieved the Government of their immediate anxieties, and the subject was dismissed. Even Sir Louis Mallet, in December, 1866, though he was far-seeing enough to express the fear that "the future course of silver is very uncertain, and thus all foundation for our financial calculations is wanting," had not at that time grasped the situation as he afterwards did. He spoke of "the utter collapse of the Silver Question" as if a settlement had been arrived at.

It was not till the Report of the Gold and Silver Commission was issued that the fundamental cause of the disturbance was thoroughly understood and explained to the people of this country. The origin of the evil was then ascertained to be the break-up of the Bimetallic System in Europe and in the United States. That system had, up to 1873, maintained "a link between silver and gold which had kept the price of the former, as measured by the latter, constant, at about the legal ratio; and when this link was broken the silver market was open to the influence of all the factors which go to effect the price of a commodity." Such was the unanimous finding of the twelve Royal Commissioners appointed "to inquire into the recent changes in the relative values of the precious metals." This discovery at once let in a flood of light on the Indian Currency Question, which, so far from being disposed of, as the Indian Government thought in 1876, had reappeared between that year and 1888 in an aggravated and more acute form.

Most people would have supposed that after this revelation the natural course for the British Government to pursue would have been to take steps, or, at any rate, to encourage steps being taken, to re-establish the "link between gold and silver" which had been broken, and so rehabilitate the finances and place the trade of India upon a sound and permanent foundation. Successive Indian Governments had urged this even before the authoritative deliverance of the Royal Commission had been pronounced.

In 1881, while the Monetary Conference was sitting in Paris, the Government of India took up definite ground. Referring to a proposal, which was actually made to the Conference, that if a Bimetallic Union were formed, India should engage to keep her mints open to silver so long as the convention of other nations remained in force, the Indian Government proceeded to say in a despatch, dated June 10 in that year: "Should, however, no alternative present itself between allowing any international arrangement to break down, and pledging India to join the Bimetallic Union, we are of opinion that we should be justified in going a step further. Under these circumstances we should be prepared to recommend that India should join the Bimetallic Union if a sufficiently large number of other Governments were prepared to join." This proposal was not laid before the Conference.

Again, in 1886, this subject was brought before the Home Government by Lord Dufferin and his colleagues. In a despatch, dated Calcutta, February 2, 1886, they say: "The establishment of a fixed ratio between gold and silver is not beyond the possibility of human control, and ordinary prudence requires that steps should be taken to remove every preventible cause of future financial embarrassment." They urge upon the Home Government the duty of "taking the initiative in promoting a Conference for the consideration of remedial measures." They add: "Recent events have brought into greater prominence the evils with which the world is threatened by the state of the currency in the United States of America and in the countries comprised in the Latin Union, and the present time would appear to be a favourable one for re-opening the whole question. Even if your Lordship" (this was addressed to Lord Randolph Churchill, who was then Secretary of State for

India) "see no prospect of immediate success, we should still recommend that the question be raised again. The evils connected with the present state of affairs are so serious that the adoption, sooner or later, by international agreement, of measures which will bring about a stable ratio between gold and silver, appears to us to be only a question of time. A wide and general discussion of the question is essential to the formation of a body of public opinion sufficient to enforce a final settlement, and the sooner a final settlement is taken in hand the easier it will be to carry out, and the more satisfactory to all concerned will be the result."

In September, 1886, the Government of the day appointed the Royal Commission on Gold and Silver. That Commission endorsed most of the views which had been put forward by the Government of India, though in the end one section of the Commission hesitated to recommend that this country should join a Bimetallic Union. Since the date of that Report (1888), however, Mr. Leonard Courtney, one member of that section, has severed himself from his colleagues on this point, and, impressed by what has since occurred, has publicly given his support to the desirability of an international agreement. In the April Number of *The Nineteenth Century* this year he wrote: "Five years ago I joined with my friends in deprecating any attempt to establish an international agreement for the free coinage of both gold and silver as standard money. I have advanced with further experience and reflection to the belief that such an agreement is to be desired."

Thus a majority of the Royal Commissioners are now in favour of an International Bimetallic Agreement for the establishment of a Joint Standard.

This solution of the Indian difficulty has since 1881 been the one advocated by the Government of India. In 1892, in a despatch, dated March 23, they say: "We are desirous, as we have always been, of aiding in the settlement of the Silver Question by international agreement."

Sir David Barbour, Finance Minister of India, in his Minute attached to the Correspondence, and which contains the proposal for a gold standard for India, laid before Lord Herschell's Committee, says in unmistakable terms, "I have no hesitation in saying that an international agreement for the free coinage of both silver and gold, and for the making of them full legal tender at a fixed ratio, would be far better for India and all other countries than the establishment of the single gold standard, even if the latter course be possible."

" With regard to the question of the expediency of attempting to introduce a gold standard into India, I do not go further than saying that if a general agreement for the free coinage of both silver and gold at a ratio cannot be obtained, and if the United States does not adopt free coinage of silver, I think an attempt should be made to establish a gold standard in this country."

It is well-known that the Indian Currency Association likewise supports an International Bimetallic Agreement as the best solution of the question, if the Home Government could be induced to sanction it.

From this review it is manifest that the closing of the Mints to silver in India, or the establishment of a gold standard, either with or without a gold currency in that country, so far as these measures have been at any time suggested by the Indian authorities, must be regarded as desperate alternatives, only justifiable if the Home Government obstinately refused to adopt the only safe and sound remedy of international agreement.

It is but fair to the Indian Government that their position in .his matter should be clearly understood. The responsibility of the step which has just been taken does not rest with them. Whatever difficulties or dangers, either in India or in this country, come in its train, the blame must rest entirely with the Government at home, which has persistently ignored the primary recommendation of its responsible advisers in India.

No one who reads the Report of "The Committee appointed to enquire into the Indian Currency" can fail to see that they were deliberately placed by the British Government in such a position that they could only register and endorse one conclusion.

In the first place, the question submitted to them was of a most limited character. A Correspondence between the Government of India and the Secretary of State for India in Council was laid before the Committee. In the forefront of that Correspondence was placed, in the strongest language, the recommendation that the settlement of the Silver Question should be attained by international agreement. Yet that proposal is not referred to the Committee at all by the Secretary of State. Their attention is confined entirely to the alternative and subsidiary "proposal for stopping the free coinage of silver in India, with a view to the introduction of a gold standard." It is admitted by Lord Kimberley, in his communication to Lord Herschell, that the effect of this measure, if adopted, "will by no means be confined to India." Yet the Government deliberately ignore and forbid all consideration by the Committee of other proposals which the Government of India had been repeatedly urging upon England for ten or twelve years, as the only safe and rational method of relieving India from the grave difficulties in her finance and her trade, with which she had been forced to struggle in consequence of the heavy fall in the gold price of silver. Lord Kimberley suggests that the question before the Committee will be whether there is sufficient ground for "over-ruling" the Government of India in the second and alternative pro-posal which the pressing conditions of Indian finance compelled them to submit, but which they did not like. He does not allow Lord Herschell and his colleagues to consider the more important and primary question whether there is sufficient ground for "over-ruling" the Government of India on the main proposal which they did like, and they had for years recommended.

This proceeding of itself shows the limited duty which the Com-mittee was summoned to perform.

Again, the composition of the Committee was unfortunate. It is true that, of the men chosen, some were able and experienced in official life, while others were learned in economic science. But there was an entire absence of any representation of Eastern Banking, or of Commerce or Industry, either Indian or British. These interests were quite as much at stake in the decision to which the Committees should come, and were at least quite as im-portant, as the financial position of the Government of India, or the pecuniary difficulties of the civil and military services in that country. No doubt evidence was accepted from merchants and others engaged in Indian trade. But it will be found, when the details of the Report are examined, that little weight was given by the Committee to this evidence, which was almost unanimous in condemning the action which was contemplated, and which was subsequently adopted.

The Report itself is an interesting, and in many ways an instruc-tive, document. But it is unsatisfactory for two reasons. In the first place, because its scope is so narrow; and, in the second place, because a foregone conclusion manifestly dominates all the argu-ments and examination of facts which it contains.

The great object to be attained was the restoration of a par of exchange between the Standard money of India and the Standard money of England: in other words, between silver and gold. But this broad, paramount issue, was not submitted to the Committee at all. On the contrary, its attention was confined to one narrow, sub-sidiary proposal, which had practically been decided upon, unless the Committee absolutely rejected it,—viz., "stopping the free coin-age of silver in India with a view to the introduction of a gold stan-dard." This fact, no doubt, to a great extent explains the meagre and incomplete character of the Report, and so far as their hands were tied, the Committee cannot be held responsible.

But we now come to the work of the Committee within the limits assigned to them. The plan which they have approved is "The closing of the Mints against the free coinage of silver, accompanied by an announcement that, though closed to the public, they will be used by Government for the coinage of rupees in exchange for gold at a ratio to be then fixed (say) 1s. 4d. per rupee; and that at the Government treasuries gold will be received in satisfaction of public dues at the same ratio."

The immediate effect of this plan (now carried out) is that India at the present moment has no Standard Money at all. It possesses only an inconvertible token coinage,—nothing better in fact than a system of inconvertible paper. On the one hand the rupee is divorced from the silver which it contains ; and on the other it cannot be regarded as a fraction of the gold sovereign, for it lacks convertibility.

But it may be said this is only an intermediate step. The ultimate intention is " the introduction of a gold standard." The question then arises, How is a gold standard to be introduced, and when ? This final step seems left altogether to chance. Sir David Barbour, in his able Minute, lays down the principle that, " In order that the gold standard may be effective," not only must a limit be placed upon the number of the silver coins, but also "they must be convertible into gold coins whenever any person wishes for gold coins in exchange for silver coins."

The Committee do not appear to have attached the slightest weight to this fundamental condition. The only attempt at justification for ignoring this great principle in the science of money is to be found in the following sentence : " It must, however, be remembered that, although a nation possessed of a fairly-satisfactory monetary system might well hesitate to exchange it, even temporarily for an inconvertible currency, yet India already labours under difficulties the gravity of which is admitted."

The recommendation of the Committee, in fact, is that India should " walk out of the frying-pan into the fire."

It is not surprising, therefore, that Lord Farrer and Sir Reginald Welby should protest against this happy-go-lucky monetary system, and recommend in a note that the Government of India should at once take definite steps to " accumulate a sufficient reserve of gold to secure the convertibility of their token silver currency." How and when this is to be achieved these authorities do not state.

Sir David Barbour says : " The accumulation of a sufficient store of gold would be a measure too expensive for a country situated as India is, and when it had been accumulated and the exchangeability of the silver coins for gold coins had been guaranteed by means of it, there would be a very great risk of the whole stock of gold being drawn away in exchange for silver rupees. If this should happen,— and I think it would happen unles our stock of gold was very large indeed,—the gold standard would cease to exist, and we should find ourselves exactly where we started."

But the Committee, from the nature of the case, could scarcely be expected to deal with inconvenient questions of this kind on broad lines. They had a mandate to sanction, if possible, the closing of the Mints to silver, unless they were convinced that such a measure would produce an immediate catastrophe.

Mr. Leonard Courtney plaintively regrets that he was not allowed to raise "previous questions," though he held there were preliminary questions which ought "first to be determined." Under these circumstances the Committee boldly set themselves to minimize all the objections to the limited and indefinite proposal which had been submitted for their consideration.

Out of twenty-seven witnesses who were examined none appear to have advocated the measure on the ground of its own intrinsic merits. Objection after objection was raised by experienced Indian authorities, by bankers, by merchants, and by economists. But these objections are as a rule dealt with in a most perfunctory manner in the Report. The future of silver is left out of account altogether. On this point the Report states that "all the factors of the problem are so uncertain that it is impossible to predict with any confidence, or in numerical terms, what the effect of closing the Mints would be on the value of uncoined silver." As to "the future value or gold price of the rupee" the Committee are equally vague. "There might be some time to wait before there was any increase in its value. . . Neither could we trace the progress of the enhancement of the value of the rupee in respect of time or place which we should expect to follow the closings of the Mints."

The Report contains an elaborate and most interesting statement of the "Different Currency Systems of different nations." But when the Committee give the "general conclusion" at which they arrive, after a careful examination of these systems, it is most disappointing. They merely say : "On the whole it seems to us that, whilst the differences we have pointed out prevent the cases of the countries referred to from being applicable in all respects as precedents to the case of India, and the circumstances of each particular country must be studied, yet the experience derived from the currencies of those countries is not without value as bearing on the questions which we have to consider, and is important as showing under what various conditions the exchange value of a currency may be maintained."

The only real "general conclusion" which it is possible to draw from that part of the Report which deals with the "Effect of the Proposals," is that in the opinion of the Committee it is "a leap in the dark," and that none of its results can possibly be estimated till the experiment has been made.

The way in which the Committee deal with the objections urged by the witnesses whom they examined is more curious still. Most of these objections are admitted to be of great weight. All that the Committee venture to say, in reply to them, is that possibly they are not entitled to so much weight as the objectors think.

It may be useful to give a short synopsis of the answers of the Committee to the most important of these objections.

1. "Spurious Coinage."—"It is difficult to estimate with precision the real extent of the alleged danger; but when it is borne in mind that in order to carry out operations on an extended scale expensive and specially-constructed machinery would be requisite, we doubt whether the danger of India being flooded with a large amount of spurious coin would really be a grave one."

2. "Effect on Hoards of Silver."—"It cannot, we think, be doubted that the closing of the Mints would in this case depreciate the silver ornaments and the uncoined silver hoarded by the people of India. Such a use of ornaments is, however, said to be rare."

3. "Burden of Taxation would be Increased."—"The argument is no doubt sound; but there are answers to this objection which have no little weight."

The "answers" are not given!

4. "Alternative of Increased Taxation."—"Supposing the choice to be between an indirect increase of taxation arising from arrest of the fall in the value of the rupee, or even from a considerable increase in its value on the one hand, and the imposition of new taxation on the other, the latter of these courses would be far more likely to lead to popular discontent and political difficulty than the former."

If this argument is worth anything, it means that the people of India are in the future to have increased taxation imposed upon them in an insidious form, in the hope that they may not discover it. Hitherto they have enjoyed a stable standard of value, of which they are now to be deprived, under which prices have remained practically stable, while gold prices have seriously fallen.

5. "Trade with Silver-using Countries."—"The proposal of the Government of India, in so far as it rendered the exchange between India and gold-using countries stable, would introduce into the trade of India with silver-using countries the same disquieting influences which it is alleged at present hamper the trade of India with gold-using countries. It must, however, be observed that the trade of India with silver-using countries only amounts to about half of her trade with gold-using countries."

One-third of the trade of India evidently is of no consequence! But a more definite answer to the objection is attempted,—viz., "That the Indian produce imported into China is paid for ultimately by goods exported by China to other countries, and that, *if* the gold prices of these commodities does not fall owing to a fall in the gold value of silver, they would realize a higher silver price, and that China would thus be able to pay a higher price for the Indian imports. We have already given our reasons for doubting whether the fall in the gold price of silver does operate to any considerable extent in reducing the gold price of commodities exported from silver-using countries."

It will be observed that the validity of this answer depends entirely upon an "if," and a very doubtful "if" too !

6. "TRADE OF INDIA IN COMPETITION WITH SILVER-USING COUNTRIES."—"Another objection strongly urged is that, if the proposal of the Government were carried out, and there should arise a great divergence between the ratio borne to gold by the rupee and by silver respectively, this would seriously affect the trade of India with silver-using countries, and stimulate in those countries the production of commodities which compete with Indian commodities in the markets of the world, and that the effect of such increased competition would be seriously felt by India." The answer of the Committee to this argument is that " China is slow to move."

If the Consular reports are to be trusted, China has already moved. But, whatever may be said of China, the people of Japan, at any rate, are sure to be on the alert, and will move rapidly.

7. "OPIUM TRADE WITH CHINA."—"The amount imported from India forms only a small portion of the total consumption. Indian opium is in truth a luxury; its use in preference to Chinese opium is a matter of taste, and depends on its real or assumed superior qualities. Under these circumstances, it may be doubted whether any considerable diminution in the rupee value of opium exports to China would be likely to result from the adoption of the proposals of the Indian Government."

8. "COMPETITION OF SILVER-USING COUNTRIES WITH INDIA IN OTHER MARKETS."—"But, allowing that the argument of those who raise the objection with which we have been dealing is not without foundation, consideration of the experience derived from a study of the history of Indian exports during the period characterized by a fall in the gold value of silver, as noticed in paragraph 27, leads us to doubt whether the suggested advantage is not much less than those who urge the argument suppose."

9. "TEA PLANTATIONS."—"It cannot be denied that if the proposed currency change were adopted in India alone its tendency

might be for a time to benefit the producer in Ceylon, and, perhaps, the Chinese in his competition with the Indian. To what extent this tendency would prejudice the Indian producer it is impossible to forecast, and, even so far as it did so, it must be remembered that it would not necessarily entail disadvantage on the country as a whole; and having regard to the history of the Indian tea trade, and to its great progress in recent years under existing conditions, we cannot think it likely that any very serious prejudice would result."

10. "China might Produce what She now Imports from India."—"To this it is replied, and we think with force, that the want of railways and other means of communication in China, the heavy and arbitrary imposts to which production is thus subjected, and other causes, deprive these apprehensions of any very serious foundation."

Thus, it will be seen that the Committee do not deny the cogency of most of these objections. They content themselves, however, with vague answers, taking an optimist view of results, and attaching no real weight to the opinions and arguments of the witnesses whom they themselves had selected as experts.

There are, moreover, two obvious fallacies which they adopt, and which vitiate their reasoning in several portions of the Report.

The first of these is the assumption that the Indian producer has received a higher silver price for his produce, so that the fall in exchange has benefited him. This is (to say the least of it) very disputable. Indeed, though they proceed on this theory in more than one of their arguments, they themselves are obliged to admit that, even if true at all, it is only lately, and partially, that silver prices in India have risen. In paragraph 31 they say: " Down to a comparatively late date it was generally believed that, notwithstanding a fall in the gold value of silver, prices in India had been practically unaltered; but the evidence before us points to the conclusion that during recent years the silver price of Indian produce has risen." The evidence referred to in this paragraph is not given, so there is no opportunity afforded for testing it. But, even if it be a fact that prices have risen recently, the causes of that rise would have to be examined before any conclusions could be based upon the statement. In any case, the broad fact remains, even in the view of the Committee, that for nearly twenty years, while gold prices have fallen as much as thirty per cent., silver prices have practically remained unaltered, showing that silver is a more stable standard of value than gold.

The second fallacy is that the fall in the gold price of silver has had no effect in reducing the gold price of commodities. It is to be noticed that, though the Committee use this assumption in reply to the objections that the manufacturer in India will suffer serious loss in his trade with China and other silver-using countries, if the rupee is kept artificially at a higher value than the market value of the silver contained in it, and argue that the rupee price of manufactures in India will be maintained, they do not undertake to deny that the gold prices of manufactures in this country have been driven down by the fall in exchange. They simply say " the allegation is strongly controverted," and then they proceed to argue as if it had been disproved.

But a still more unfortunate feature in the Committee's Report is the absence of any apparent realization on the part of Lord Herschell and his colleagues (except, perhaps, Mr. Courtney) of the revolution outside India which a decision in favour of closing the Indian Mints would create. Though warned by Lord Kimberley that the effect of this measure, if adopted, would " by no means be confined to India," there is no reference in the Report to its probable consequences to the investing, trading, or industrial classes in England, much less to other consequences which might flow from it in America or on the Continent of Europe.

Yet these consequences must ultimately be very grave. Already in the City it is said that there has been a shrinkage in the value of securities of no less than £28,000,000, accompanied by many failures. It is pointed out in a carefully reasoned article in *The Statist*, of July 15, that, though so far as the India Council succeeds in fixing the value of the rupee, exports from England to India may be temporarily stimulated, the probability is that ultimately the effect will be that India's power to buy will be greatly reduced, and that Lancashire and other industrial centres will in the end lose considerably more than they are likely to gain.

What the effect in the United States and on the Continent may be it is difficult to forecast. But, at any rate, this is certain : The closing of the Mints in India is a deliberate blow to silver, and will discourage its use as a standard of value, or even as a monetary metal. Moreover, it indicates a policy in direct opposition to the united opinion of the nations lately assembled in Conference at Brussels, and is in direct violation of the principles laid down in the instructions given to the British delegates appointed to attend that Conference.

No reference is made to these important matters in the Report of Lord Herschell's Committee. The omission is remarkable, and it shows the " parochial spirit " in which the investigation of this grave subject of world-wide interest has been conducted.

More remarkable still is the complete silence of the Committee on the appreciation of gold, and the bearing which the establishment of a gold standard in India may have upon this vital question.

It may be that a majority of the members of the Committee disbelieve in the possibility of gold appreciation, and therefore they may have closured any reference to so pestilent a "heresy." But, unless this is the case, it seems extraordinary that in sanctioning a policy and a plan which, if it is to be successful at all, must sooner or later entail a new demand for gold as a reserve to secure the convertibility of the token rupee, not the slightest consideration, or, at any rate, not the slightest expression of opinion, should have been given as to the effect of this new demand upon the value of the Standard metal in gold-using countries, or upon gold prices. This aspect of the question is indeed important as regards India herself; for, if a gold standard is to be forced upon her, she will become vitally concerned in any variations in her new measure of value. If henceforth both her internal and external trade is to be based upon gold prices, instead of, as hitherto, upon silver prices, any appreciation of gold will have a meaning for her and an influence on her future condition which the Committee were bound to take into their consideration. But they do not seem to have done so, or if they have, they have not allowed the world to know what was the result of their deliberations.

The Report as a whole is scarcely worthy of the eminent men who framed it. No doubt they were placed in a false position. The task imposed upon them was a difficult one, and the conditions under which they were called upon to undertake it made it more difficult still. They were not allowed to choose the gap in the hedge, which the Indian Government had pointed out as the safest course. They were compelled to take the fence at the point where it was the "blindest." No wonder they floundered.

The future of this question is still as uncertain as ever. No settlement has been arrived at. Those who objected most to "tampering with the currency" have been the first to tamper with it. But, unfortunately, they have only been able so far to abolish one system, without establishing any other in its place. What that other system is to be no one knows. The hope is that, now that Monometallists have done their worst in destroying the old house, scientific builders may, before it is too late, be called in to construct a durable edifice on a sound foundation.

WILLIAM H. HOULDSWORTH.

# Institute of Bankers.

## JANUARY, 1894.

Thomas Salt, Esq., a Vice-President, in the Chair.

## THE REPORT OF THE INDIAN CURRENCY COMMITTEE.

### By Sir Richard Temple, Bart., M.P., G.C.S.I.

[Read before the Institute, on Wednesday, December 6th].

HAVE the pleasure to comply with your request to address you, briefly, on the subject of the Report of the Indian Currency Committee of the present year. In attempting this, however, I will, with your permission, avoid the expression of any opinion on what is known as the bimetallic controversy—though I may be obliged, here and there, to approach the fringe of that subject.

The contents of that Report are doubtless, in their substance, well known to you. But I must recapitulate them in a few words in order to make my comments effective. The conclusion of the Committee runs thus :—" They cannot, in view of the serious evils " with which the Government of India may, at any time, be confronted, " if matters are left as they are, advise the Secretary of State to " overrule the proposals for the closing of the Mints and the adoption " of a gold standard, which that Government have submitted. But " they consider that the closing of the Mints against the free coinage " of silver should be accompanied by an announcement that, though " closed to the public, they will be used by Government for the " coinage of rupees in exchange for gold at a ratio of 1s. 4d. per " rupee, and that, at the Government treasuries, gold will be received " in satisfaction of public dues, at the same ratio."

This was dated the 31st of May last, 1893, and, on the 26th of June, it was announced in the House of Commons that the Government of India had acted upon this Report, exactly on the above terms. The Government added :—" It is intended to introduce a gold standard " into India, but gold will not be made a legal tender at present."

Upon this Report, then, the following questions arise : 1. What was the action of the Government of India ? 2. How is that to be justified ?   3. What is its effect on the exchange between India and England ?   4. How does it affect the Indian trade ?   5. How does it concern the interests of the natives of India, apart from their commercial interests ?   6. What is the history of this question in India ?   7. Was there any alternative other than that which has been adopted ?

These questions are bound up together. To treat them properly, would require, not one address, but a series of addresses. Therefore if, owing to exigency of time, I touch on them imperfectly, I must hope to be excused.

In regard to the first question, the Government of India passed an Act through their legislature closing the Mints against the free coinage of rupees, and so far modifying the legal right which the public had of presenting silver to be thus coined. This was the main action, of which the consequences would be immediate. The amount of such new coinage, during the preceding ten years, had stood at eighty-two millions of tens of rupees, or over eight millions a year. This coinage would now cease. Such cessation, by rendering rupees more scarce than before, must raise their value in a greater or less degree. But there was a further proceeding, namely, the offer to take gold in exchange for silver at the rate of 1s. 4d. for the rupee. The consequences of this were not likely to be immediate. But it had a particular influence on the public mind, because it apparently indicated the aim of the Government to determine the rate of exchange at 1s. 4d. for the rupee. The ulterior policy was, no doubt, to pave the way for the introduction of a gold currency as legal tender. The immediate intention was to steady the value of the rupee, and to prevent its continuing in a descending scale. But evidently this would, on the other hand, prevent it ascending, and so disturbing the arrangements of trade. Thus, the growing loss of exchange, and the drain on the resources of the Indian Government, would be arrested. But the Government did not go so far as to try to force the rupee up to 1s. 4d., although this was a very low rate compared with that which had for at least a century been regarded as normal. The low rate was indicated, with a view to approximation, towards the existing status, and to the avoidance of trouble in mercantile arrangements. There was no thought of restoring the rupee to its former value. nor any hope of reverting to the exchange which had prevailed for several generations, up to the year 1870 or 1872.

The second question is how can this action be justified ? The answer to that will in the first place depend on the opinion you may form as to whether this artificial raising of the value of the rupee—for such it actually is—must be held to be in principle objectionable. I know not how the adherents of the bimetallic theory can consistently say that such is the case. Some bimetallic authorities do, I know, object to what has been done. They may urge that the measure is so imperfect as to be worse than useless, and so forth. Some among them perhaps think that the rate of 1*s.* 4*d.* is so low as to prejudice or even compromise the cause of silver generally. I do not undertake to enter on those opinions. But I suppose that the majority of those present will consider that this interference with the value of the rupee is *per se* objectionable in principle. I do not at all deny that it is so. But then comes the question what is the justification? The fall in exchange going on for full twenty years, had been from the beginning burdensome. Still India had prospered, and in all other respects her finances had flourished. So for some time the Government of India endured the burden without seriously complaining, and without adopting any drastic measures. But within the last decade, its endurance had been strained almost to breaking, as the case grew worse and worse. Within the last year or two years, a crisis was evidently approaching when some abnormal effort must be made, and some drastic measure adopted. When political or administrative evils are considered, we must ever remember that an unsound measure of finance may be as great an evil as any; and among its faults there may be this, that while it does all the harm that may have been feared from it in some directions, it fails to do the good expected of it in the direction that was intended. Granted, then, the evil of such a measure, it has to be weighed against the alternative evils that presented themselves. These were either the continual devising of new taxes, the augmenting of old taxes, the ensuing unpopularity, discontent and political ill-feeling,—on the one hand ; or else the repeated cutting down of the civil administration with the consequent losses and disadvantages, the reduction of military strength, with the accompanying insecurity—on the other hand. The adoption of such fiscal measures in time of peace, thereby using up all the resources available for warlike or other emergency—was that from which any government would shrink. The imperial peril arising from a wholesale reduction of establishments was one which no government would voluntarily incur. Economy is, of course, always possible, but no ordinary economy would meet the difficulties of the case. Well, then, measure for measure, weighing evil against evil, can we wonder that the Government adopted the monetary expedient, although it was unsound in principle? Surely, in monetary and financial crises, the government in other countries has taken steps, not strictly justifiable in principle. Is it not natural that the Indian Government did the same, when confronted with extreme danger, political and administrative? There are objectors whose opinions we respect, and whose arguments cannot be gainsaid, who denounce the unsound measure actually adopted. But they have invariably failed to show how the Government could afford to do nothing, or how, if it was to do anything, it could have done other than what it actually did.

There was this further argument for what the Government did, and that was the force of all that public opinion in India, which concerns itself in these matters. There was the agitation by Currency associations specially formed ; there was the unanimous sentiment of the several Chambers of Commerce ; there was the Report of the Committee of the highest experts in England, in the same sense. In the face of the opinion of the commercial and financial world around it, the Government could not have disregarded such a Report, even if it had been so minded, which, indeed, it was not.

Lastly, there was urgency in the demand for a decision. It was known that the newly-elected President of the United States and his government would urge a change in the currency, which might involve the repeal of the legislation comprised in the Bland and Sherman Acts. The repeal might cause such a further fall in silver as would add to the embarrassments surrounding any course that the Government might take. Subsequently, this repeal has, indeed, taken place, and, notwithstanding that, the expected drop in the price of silver has not as yet occurred. But the Government, in June last, could not have ventured to anticipate this, it being too good to hope for. And it may yet occur after all.

The third question is, what effect has this action on the exchange between England and India ? Before the month of June last, 1893, when the mints were closed, the exchange had fallen to a little over 1s. 2d. for the rupee, with the prospect of a still further fall. The Secretary of State in London had sold council bills on the Indian Treasury as low as 1s. 2¾d., of course, with grievous financial disadvantage. Immediately after the closing of the mints it rose to over 1s. 4d., but fell almost immediately. The Secretary of State being unable to obtain suitable tenders, sold hardly any council bills for several months, making other arrangements for supplying his needs in London. It was held by some that the Secretary of State should declare an intention of not accepting any tenders for less than a certain rate, the desired rate being 1s. 4d. But the Secretary of State made no such declaration. On the other hand, he did not press his invitation for tenders, there being doubt as to whether any suitable tenders could be obtained. It was hoped that as the winter, which is the active season in India, should approach, the sale of council bills would begin again, and such is proving to be the case.

A beginning was made, for nearly one million of tens of rupees worth of council bills were sold. But this process has become checked—as "a false dawn"—and application is to be made to Parliament for power to raise a loan of ten millions sterling, in England, to meet the current needs of the year, if the demand for bills at acceptable rates shall not revive.

Meanwhile, from June, 1893 (the time of closing the mints), up to the present time, December, the exchange has ranged between 1s. 3¾d., an abnormal rate, and 1s. 2¾d. ; but for the most part has been steady at 1s. 3d. to 1s. 3¼d. We may say, then, that whereas before June there was a tendency to fall below even a deep depreciation, there has since June been comparative steadiness, with a tendency to rise, though we are yet far from the contemplated standard of 1s. 4d. This modicum of result is for the present attributable to the closing of the mints, and though it may be small, still the comparative steadiness, the arrest of the decline, may be regarded as benefits. It is, of course, impossible to say whether this effect will last.

On the other hand, while the rate of exchange and the current value of the rupee have been steadied, the price of uncoined or bar silver has fallen since the action of the Government of India indicating the relation of cause and effect. The fall is in this wise. Before the closing of the mints the price was 38 pence an ounce, and is now but little over 32 pence; representing a fall of 16 per cent. We cannot as yet say what the effect, if any, of this will be upon the trade. It does, *pro tanto*, depreciate the mass of uncoined silver hoarded by the natives, and to that point I shall advert presently.

The fourth question is, how does this concern the trade internal and external of India? And I assume that the banking interest being bound up with the commercial interest, whatever helps the one must help the other or *vice versa*. It is believed that heretofore the natives have not suffered from the fall in the value of silver, their legal tender being in that metal, the appreciation of gold has not troubled them; the determination of the relative value of the two metals has never been in their thoughts; they are for the most part, though not wholly, unconcerned in the monetary controversies that have agitated Europe and America. They have seen within the present generation great changes in the purchasing power of the rupee, that is, in the range of prices—but these are attributed to material and economic causes quite apart from the value of silver. The foreign trade is not thought to have suffered thereby, at least, up to very recent years. Indeed, the export trade is believed by some to have actually benefited. As silver is, so to speak, a mechanism for the due conduct of trade, and for the transaction of commerce, then the cheapness of that article may afford at least a temporary stimulus to commerce. And that particular benefit accruing to their own productions, would come home to the natives. So far, has this view been carried by some authorities, that the prosperity of this, the greatest branch of the foreign trade, and the consequent increase in the public revenues, have been ascribed in part to the cheapness of silver, and all this has been adduced as a set-off against the embarrassments which the Government has suffered from the depreciation of the rupee.

Until recently, the Chambers of Commerce had not complained. Recently, however, they have joined in the complaints made by all the European interests connected with the Government. The strong ground of complaint has been the difficulty of making bargains for any length of time, owing to the uncertainty in the value of silver.

It may be well here to consider what is the origin of council bills. The foreign trade of India may be reckoned at 197 millions of tens of rupees in annual value. The exports of 113½ millions considerably exceed the imports of 83¼ millions. There is consequently a balance of 30 millions in favour of India which has to be made up by remittances. In other words, for her exports of produce India is paid partly by manufactured articles and partly by remittances.

There is, however, a further element in the case. The Government of India has to pay to England a debt of about 16 to 18 millions sterling annually, for the discharge of which it is obliged to raise the vast sum of rupees which has proved so embarrassing. Now this helps to balance the trade as above set forth. England owes India, say, 30 millions of tens of rupees a year for produce, after striking the balance of imports and exports. But then India owes England 16 to 18 millions sterling annually. This latter obligation is a set-off against the former.

In order to avoid the transmission of silver in bulk to India by the merchants, and the return of that silver by the Government there to England, the practice is to buy in London, and transmit to India, council bills—that is, they pay so many sovereigns into the treasury of the Secretary of State in London, and receive in return so many rupees from the treasury in India. Thus the Secretary of State is said to sell his council bills, and the rate at which he can do this is a large factor in determining the exchange between England and India. It follows that these bills will be in demand according as the balance to be made up is greater or smaller. Thus, whatever stimulates the export trade, must promote the demand for council bills, and so tend to raise their price to the advantage of the Government.

Now, before the recent action of the Government, the cheapening of silver helped the export trade. But, although that action has caused silver to fall, and has *pro tanto* cheapened the metal, yet the actual advantage to that branch of trade which most nearly concerns these monetary arrangements may be doubted. For this cheapening has been effected only by the separation of the value of silver from the value of the rupee. Now though a merchant may buy his silver in London more cheaply than before, yet I apprehend that, when the metal arrives in India, its value for trade purposes will have to be adjusted in rupees. Thus the Government, while rendering silver cheaper, has rendered the rupee dearer, and the one consideration counterbalances the other.

But, further, the surplus of Indian merchandise exports over imports has been steadily falling. Between April and September it fell from 5½ millions of tens of rupees to less than one million. In October actually there was no surplus at all, but, on the contrary, a slight balance of ¼ of a million the other way. The returns are not made up for November, but, probably, there is no marked improvement. All this accounts for there being no demand for council bills, as there is no balance due to India to be remitted.

Again, the surplus of Indian silver imports, which rose for a special reason in July last, has since been maintained from ¾ of a million of tens of rupees to 1⅛ millions. The probable reason being that people are sending out silver wherewith to buy up rupees in the Indian markets instead of sending it to Indian mints to be coined. Thus rupees will probably become dearer than before.

Lastly, deducting treasure gold and silver from merchandise, the net balance in favour of India fell from 4½ millions of tens of rupees in April to 2¾ millions in June. Then, from July onwards, the balance has disappeared, there actually being a balance against India of ½ a million of tens of rupees in July, and a balance of nearly 1¾ millions in October. Thus the ordinary balance of trade has been temporarily reversed—no remittances are required to be made, and, consequently, there has been no demand for council bills. Doubtless, the reversal may in some degree be attributed to the action of the Government regarding the currency.

There may be anxiety lest the cessation of silver coinage should cause inconvenience to trade, inasmuch as 8 millions of tens of rupees have, of late years, been issued annually on the average from the mints. The total active circulation is estimated at 115 millions of tens of rupees. The annual coinage partly keeps this circulation up, and partly supplies the native hoards. No inconvenience from the cessation, however, appears as yet to be felt, because some 2½ millions of tens of rupees' worth of silver were on their way to India when the mints were closed, and have been admitted to coinage. Moreover, there has been increased activity in the mints of several native states, where coins, though not legal tender, are of the same standard value as British coins.

Subsidiary to the specie there is the Government paper currency. In the years 1890 to 1892, it rose from 16 to 29 millions of tens of rupees, attributable to silver imports resulting from the Sherman Act in America. It afterwards fell to 26 millions, but now stands again at 29 millions, large shipments having been made to India shortly before the mints were closed, and having been subsequently coined in exchange for notes. Now, if more circulating medium shall be needed, owing to the closing of the mints, that need may be supplied by paper currency. It must, however, be remembered that beyond a legal limit of 8 millions of tens of rupees which may be issued without metallic reserve, all notes issued must be in return for gold or silver coin. Now such additional issue, if made against silver, will not relieve the scarcity of rupees, but it may have that effect if made against gold, and people may tender that at the rate of 1s. 4d. for the rupee.

There is yet one point, namely this. It was foreseen that the depreciation of silver relatively to the rupee would give an advantage to other silver using countries such as China trading with or competing against India. Such indeed was the effect at first, notably with the opium and the piece goods exported from India to China. The effect is, however, not expected to be permanent, and the check in the piece goods trade is partly attributed to over production, irrespective of the price of silver. In short, while the steadiness of exchange, produced by the action of Government, has benefited India's trade with the United Kingdom, it has temporarily damaged India's trade with the far East.

Lastly, it has been urged by some, that the cheapness of silver, by facilitating the exportation of wheat from India to England, has helped to lower and keep down the price of that article in England. Now, after what has been just set forth, I cannot deny that such may be the case to some extent. Far beyond this, however, are two cardinal and material causes, namely, the completion of the railways from the distant interior to the coast, and the opening of the Suez Canal. These are enough to account for the exportation from India to England, irrespective of lesser causes.

The fifth question is, how does this concern the interests of the people of India as apart from their commercial interests already noticed. Now herein they have a vital interest which heretofore they have not realized, namely, whatever embarrasses the Government financially must fall upon them—the subjects. Had, what is commonly termed the loss by exchange, not occurred, the Indian treasury would have been the richer by hundreds of millions of rupees, and that signifies either that taxation might have been avoided or remitted, or else that beneficent expenditure for public improvement might have been allowed. Were the so-called loss by exchange to be still further aggravated, then the Government would be driven to the severe alternatives already sketched, and these would be acutely felt by the natives. If, therefore, the action of the Government should succeed in arresting that embarrassment, no interest will be more perceptibly benefited than that of the natives. The point need not be laboured here, but it is so obvious that we may wonder why it is not more prominently noticed than it has been.

Further, the natives are very large holders of silver, both in specie and in bullion. It may be in your recollection that some years ago I presented to you a calculation, on the best data then available, showing that the silver coins of India were then valued at 333 millions sterling (at the rate of ten rupees to the sovereign). If that calculation were then correct, the sum must have since risen to nearly 400 millions. The whole of this vast sum is not used for circulation ; a large part is hoarded or used for personal ornament. Besides this, there is an untold mass of uncoined silver also used for such decoration. The sum total of coined and uncoined, is not within our knowledge, but it might conceivably amount to from 500 to 600 millions of tens of rupees. Now I have heard some authorities take the fall of silver caused by the action of the Government, apply that as a percentage to this sum total, and so reckon a loss of some few millions, and then designate this loss by severe expressions. But the argument does not apply to the coined silver which is actually appreciated, and the gain there might be set off against the depreciation of the uncoined. But this uncoined silver is chiefly used for ornament, though in time of urgency, like famine and so forth, it is pawned. Ordinarily, the holders never think of the market value of this silver. In time of famine, too, the price of grain becomes such a dominant consideration as to drive out all thought of the price of silver. Thus the supposed loss is not really felt ; but let its existence be granted, what then ? It is only the widely spread contribution of the people towards the financial deficit. And if they were asked whether they would prefer an indirect and impalpable damage of this sort to direct taxation, there is no doubt what their answer would be.

Moreover, it is late in the day to adduce any hypothetical injury to the natives from the fall in silver. For this has been going on and growing ever since 1871, between which year and 1893 silver fell 37 per cent. They have seemed to be unconscious of it, and they do not believe themselves to have suffered. Is, then, a further fall of 16 per cent. in 1893—a decline from 38*d*. per ounce to 32*d*.—such a difference as *per se* to constitute a wrong ? If they now suffer sensibly from this further decline, their sufferings must have begun some years ago, which does not, however, appear to be the case.

In connection with this, too, it has been said that the action of the Government in causing this further fall is injurious to the payers of the land tax, commonly called the ryots. I am unable to follow this argument. Certainly since 1871 the ryots have not been suffering. Between that year and the present time the land revenue has risen from 20½ millions of tens of rupees to 24 millions by natural increment, without any increase in the ratio of assessment to value of produce—an increment which absolutely represents agricultural prosperity. Shortly before 1871, prices of produce were far higher than in former times. These have been more than maintained, subsequently, and, during recent years, are found to have risen still further by 5 per cent. The means of transport and communication have multiplied, and foreign markets for produce have been opened or developed. Thus the ryot has been thriving throughout the time of the depression of silver.

The sixth question relates to the history of this question in India. I have time only to summarise this : The earliest Hindu currency was in gold with a single standard. The Mohammedans introduced silver, and in later times up to British rule there was a double standard—gold and silver. That was continued by the East India

Company's Regulation, of 1793, and lasted till 1835, when silver was declared to be the sole legal tender to an unlimited amount. In 1806, doubts of the propriety of the double standard for India were raised in England. The controversy lasted many years, and ended, as just mentioned, in 1835. On a retrospect we may now lament this, considering that gold might have then been made sole legal tender for large amounts, and silver for small amounts, as is done in England. Until 1860, no apprehension was felt; silver still commanded five shillings an ounce, the ratio of its value with gold was still fifteen to one, the rupee was still equal to two shillings. In that year, James Wilson, the famous financier, being confronted with the question of a gold standard, declared against it. The American Civil War, inflating the demand for cotton, intensified what was then called the drain of silver. Fearing lest, despite present prosperity, something untoward might happen, the Indian financiers subsequent to 1864— Sir Charles Trevelyan, Mr. Massey and myself, with the expert assistance of Sir William Mansfield (afterwards Lord Sandhurst)—did their best to introduce a gold standard into India upon the English model. The exchanges, the high price of silver, and other circumstances as they stood, say, from 1864 to 1869, presented a combination of facilities, which, if then lost, might never recur. We did our utmost for this end, but in vain. Since 1872, silver has begun to fall, till it now has but little more than half its former value. The Government of India, justly alarmed, have repeatedly urged the introduction of a gold standard, but, under existing circumstances, it is hard to see how a gold standard can be introduced without some heroic measures, which no authority is as yet prepared to recommend.

In reference to the recent offer of the Government of India, no gold has as yet been tendered—so the question of a gold currency in India remains practically as it was, and is still a matter for the future.

The seventh and last question relates to any alternative action which the Government might have taken. The only alternative needing notice here, is that of raising the seignorage of the mints in India, and imposing an import duty on silver, as being less objectionable in principle than closing the mints. This was discussed by the Committee. It has the approval of an authority of weight everywhere, but specially in this audience, namely, Sir John Lubbock. The proposal is to raise the seignorage from 2 to 10 per cent., or an increase of 8 per cent., yielding on eight millions' worth of coinage— 640,000 tens of rupees revenue—inasmuch as the 2 per cent. more than covers the cost of mintage. An import duty say, of 4 per cent. on an assumed ten millions of tens of rupees worth of imports, would yield 400,000 of tens of rupees The two items together would give a good million which certainly would be a substantial advantage to the Treasury. But it is to be remembered that according to this, coined silver would suffer a double impost. On the other hand if only one of the two imposts be taken, then the effect would not be sufficiently large. Then it might be assumed that silver would be depreciated by 12 (8 plus 4) per cent. by these two operations, and to that extent the value of silver would be separated from that of the rupee. This is somewhat less than the additional separation between the two, represented by the 16 per cent. fall in silver, already shown as having occurred since the action of the Government in June last. But then we have to reflect whether these two operations together would steady the exchange in the same way as the action of the Government has as yet steadied it. The steadying of the exchange, after all, must be the dominant consideration with the Government. We may ask ourselves, why has the exchange become steadier ? Presumably because people think that, owing to closure of the mints, rupees will be scarcer than before. Now with the alternative of the seignorage and the import duty, rupees would not be scarcer, but they would be dearer than the silver price by 12 per cent. Would that consideration steady the exchange ? This result would be more than doubtful, because the value of the rupee would still fluctuate with the price of silver. At the very best it would be less sure in its effect as compared with closing the mints. It might have been tried first, and then, if it fell short of the anticipation, the more drastic plan of closing the mints might have been resorted to. To this order of procedure there was one objection, namely, the urgency arising from the prospect of repeal of silver legislation in the United States. This would induce the Government to at once resort to the plan they deemed the more sure and efficacious, namely, closing the mints.

To conclude, I am obliged to pass over many topics connected with this great subject, such as the causes of silver being depreciated, its future prospects, and the like. I shall only add a summary of the opinions which have been submitted to you in this address, namely :—

*That* the action of the Government of India based on the Report of the Committee, though unsound in principle, was justified, indeed necessitated, by exigency ; *that* it was regulated by prudent regard to circumstances, so as to cause as little disturbance as possible to commercial contracts ; *that* as yet it has operated to steady the exchange and arrest the fall of the rupee, but its future operation is still uncertain ; *that* if things remain as they are, it will have secured, at least, a modicum of success ; *that* it is not likely to cause silver to rise considerably in value, or to rehabilitate the rupee ; *that* at present it will not injure trade by diminishing unduly the amount of the circulating medium ; *that* it will not perceptibly affect the interests of the natives who hold silver specie or bullion ; *that* the law of 1835, enacting a silver standard, is, after subsequent experience, to be regretted, but that the favouring circumstances which occurred from 1864 to 1869 for introducing a gold standard, having been passed over, are not likely to recur.

## DISCUSSION ON SIR R. TEMPLE'S PAPER.

MR. HERMANN SCHMIDT:—I hope that I may be allowed to offer my congratulations to Sir Richard Temple, for his pithy and succinct statement of that question which is probably the most important that can occupy the minds of English financiers. In listening to Sir Richard, what struck me most was the extreme reserve with which he expressed his own opinion upon the measures taken by the Indian Government. He calls it an action which is "objectionable and unsound in principle," and which has secured a "modicum of success." I cannot, however, even go as far as Sir Richard, and in support of my opinion I will place before you a few facts, in addition to the many interesting facts this paper contains. The best way of proceeding will be to take, seriatim, the seven questions raised by Sir Richard. About the first : "What was the action of the Indian Government," I need not say anything, as his account of this action is absolutely correct. The second question : "How is that to be justified," leads us to the real issue. The gist of Sir Richard's remarks *is* : necessity was its justification. This plea, however, seems to me admissible only if it can be shown that the measure adopted constitutes a real remedy, of which no proof whatever has been given. Furthermore, Sir Richard says that the evils of this measure have to be weighed against the alternative evils of devising new taxes or augmenting old taxes. But if this measure ever becomes a success, it will do so only because it was the means of an indirect and invidious augmentation of taxation. Instead of raising existing taxes, the attempt is made to insidiously raise the value of the rupee. The result is heavier taxation, the very thing which this measure is supposed to obviate. The next question : "What is its effect on the exchange between India and England," is the most important of all. Sir Richard Temple claims for this measure that it has had the effect of steadying the exchange. With all due deference to his authority, I say that, whilst the exchange has been steadied, it has not been steadied by the closing of the mints. It has been steadied by that other measure, which the Indian Government has adopted, and which has no necessary connection with the closing of the mints, and may, for the matter of that, have been adopted before the mints were closed—I mean by the suspension of the sale of the Council Bills and borrowing money in sterling. Now this last step was a most important one to take, and it has had this result, that whilst the exchange has been steadied for the traders between England and India, and for the world at large, the Indian Government has hardly derived any benefit from such steadiness because it exists only as long as the Council Bills are not pressed for sale. The fact of the matter is, the Indian Government has been paying, and is paying, for this steadiness of the exchange. If trade now benefits, it does so at the expense of the Government. Sir Richard says, " It is, of course, impossible to say whether this effect will last." To this remark I answer that it is not only possible to say that it will not last, but that it is possible to fix a limit of time beyond which it cannot last. This limit is the power of the Indian Government to borrow in sterling, and the willingness of the Indian Government to employ its credit for the purpose of steadying the exchange. I, therefore, repeat that it is wrong to represent the steadiness of the exchange as the result of closing the mints so long as you have, between the end of June and the end of November, £5,000,000 sterling of Council Bills left unsold. Sell these Bills, and, only if the exchange remains steady thereafter, can you attribute such steadiness to the closing of the mints. But I have no hesitation in stating that with £5,000,000 Council Bills thrown on the market the exchange will be very little, if at all, above the present silver parity of the rupee. Now, Sir, taking such a very different view from Sir Richard on the third question, I am bound to differ with him on the fourth : " How does it affect the Indian trade ?" Of course Sir Richard says that the Indian trade has been benefited by the steadiness of the exchange. This, however, as I have shown, is not attributable to the closing of the mints. But this steadiness of the exchange has had one very disastrous effect on which I wish to lay great stress : the destruction of the favourable balance of trade of the Indian Empire. India's balance of trade had been so steadily and so universally favourable, that no one apparently ever dreamt of its becoming adverse. Marvellous to say it has done so, and done so almost immediately after the adoption of the new monetary policy. Now this measure of the Indian Government—as well as the different schemes for a gold standard for India which have been put before this Institute—were based upon the assumption of a favourable trade balance of India. This has since disappeared—and disappeared, as Sir Richard admits, in consequence of the action of the Indian Government—and, therefore the basis of success has collapsed. I frankly admit I do not regret the change which has taken place in the commercial position of India. There is an economic school which looks upon money and its value as a matter of indifference, as a cypher for settling accounts which it would be ridiculous to think could in any way affect commerce. After the experiences in India of the last few months it will be impossible for educated men to hold this opinion any longer. I now pass to the fifth question : " How does it concern the interests of the natives of India, apart from their commercial interests ?" I quite admit that if the Government is embarrassed, the people will suffer. But if this statement is to constitute a defence for the measures of the Indian Government, it must be shown that the Government is no longer embarrassed financially. This proof is not given. Moreover, the artificial raising of the standard coin is so extraordinary a measure, and apparently only for the benefit of the Anglo-Indian element, that it is safe to say that if India were governed by native statesmen, it would never have been adopted. Believing as I do that India has derived great advantages from the dominion of England, I think everything should be done to avoid measures which are justifiable only from the standpoint of the alien and conquering race. Question number six is historical, and I will not touch upon it beyond saying that I admit there might have been a time when it was possible to introduce a gold standard into India. But this time is passed. With this we come to the last question, that of alternatives. In this connection Sir Richard mentions only one alternative and that one which it is easy for him to show will not answer. But this is not sufficient. For the fact is that already the original measures taken by the Government are admitted to have failed. These have been supplemented by borrowing in sterling, a policy which cannot be continued for ever. Additional palliatives may be decided upon, such as an import duty on silver. But I believe it will all be in vain. In the end, the Government will have to confess that on the path entered upon they cannot continue any longer. Then some other alternative than the one mentioned by Sir Richard will have to be adopted, and all I hope is that this will be done before it is too late, and before the events which are shaping themselves in India have wrought havoc and misery.

SIR JAS. L. MACKAY, K.C.I.E. : I have listened with interest to what, with all deference, I would venture to describe as the masterly address which has just been delivered. The publication of the paper will be beneficial, because, as an authority on the Indian Empire and Indian finance, there is no man living who has had such great or varied experience, or is so able to speak, as Sir Richard Temple. It is re-assuring to those who have advocated the change in the currency system of India, and it will also, I hope, be comforting to those who doubted the advisability of the change, to find that the measure which was passed into law on 26th June last, has, so far as I understand it, his general approval. The opponents of the change, naturally enough, have been disposed to point to the fact that the value of the rupee has not yet reached the figure above which it cannot rise, without fresh legislation, viz., something over 1s. 4d., but a consideration of the circumstances will explain why there has been delay in the establishment of the gold point. As far back as the Spring of 1892, there was a movement on the part of America to bring about an International Bimetallic Agreement, and, at the same time, the agitation for the reform of the currency system in India was commenced. It became evident that the time was not far distant when the Government of India would be compelled to stop the free coinage of silver, failing an international agreement, and that the result, in either case, would lead to an improvement in the gold value of the rupee. This, not unnaturally, led to speculation for the rise, resulting in the coinage of fourteen crores of rupees during the last fourteen months of the open mints in India, which amount was altogether beyond the ordinary requirements of trade. In consequence, there has been a redundancy of currency, and an absence of demand during the past six months for fresh circulating medium, the result of which has been that the Secretary of State has failed to dispose of his Council Bills. To put the case in homely words, the rupee "bulls" have been in the market to realize for the past six months, and have been competing with the Secretary of State in disposing of rupees. The absence of demand for Council Bills has also been aggravated by an exceptionally large demand for Manchester goods in India, brought about by stocks having been allowed to run extremely low during the previous twelve months, and also by the unprecedentedly cheap price of silver, which has greatly stimulated its sale in India, and led to large imports on speculation. It was unfortunate that the decision to close the Mints could not have been taken six months earlier. Had action been taken in January last, there is little doubt but that the measure would have been effective ere now. As it is, we must wait until things adjust themselves, and, in the meantime, the Secretary of State must be prepared to meet his liabilities by borrowing in England, until he is able to dispose of the rupee revenue, raised in India, at, or over, the minimum rate, under which he has lately declined to sell his drafts. There have already been indications that the redundant currency is being reduced, but it may be necessary to take steps to expedite the process, and, no doubt, the subject is receiving attention at the hands of those who are responsible for the administration of the Indian finances. It was foreseen, even by the strongest advocates of the reform, that the immediate effect might be to upset, for a time, the exports from India to silver-using countries, and this has proved to be the case, but the adjustment must come when stocks are run down in China, and the latest advices indicate that the day is not far distant when there will be a revival in the Indo-China trade. As regards opium, the anticipations of a very great decrease in the revenue from this source on the closing of the mints, have not, so far, been realized ; and the shrinkage from natural causes, which would have continued whether the mints had been closed or not, had to be faced by the Indian Government. Bar silver has been selling during the past few days, for delivery within the next few months, at a price which works out at the equivalent of a little over one shilling per rupee. With the mints closed, and without the competition of silver, the Secretary of State has been able to sell, so far, a small proportion of his requirements. Had the mints remained open, the probabilities are that he would have been able to sell none, and it was only the prospect of something being done for the rupee that enabled him to sell sufficient to meet his liabilities in the last few months of the financial year ending 31st March last. At 1s. 3¼d. exchange for the realization of £16,000,000, he requires to sell twenty-four crores of rupees; at 1s. exchange he would have to sell thirty-two crores, and the difference of eight crores, even if he had been able to sell the amount, the Government of India could not have attempted to raise by taxation without grave political danger. England declined to come to the help of India by joining in an International Bimetallic Agreement, and India was compelled to take measures to save herself. Some authorities believe that by the time India has succeeded in establishing her gold reserve, England will be so drained of the metal that she will be a suppliant for bimetallism. Others tell us that there is sufficient gold in the world for all. Years alone will prove which of these theories is the correct one. In the meantime, it is satisfactory to find that a financier and statesman, with the Indian experience of Sir Richard Temple, a man who is known to have the interest of what I might call the land of his adoption, at heart, pronounces in favour of the step taken by the Government of India on the 26th June last. I have been desired by Mr. Stephen Ralli to make the following statement on his behalf : Mr. Ralli regrets that recent indisposition prevents his being present at this meeting. He was one of those who strenuously opposed the closing of the mints in India, on the grounds, amongst others, that the step would seriously affect the export trade of the country, thus re-acting unfavourably on the import trade ; also the trade in cotton goods and opium between India and China ; and also because it would give China an unfair advantage over India, as regards tea. Now, however, that the step has been taken, Mr. Ralli considers that it is the duty of the Government to make the measure effective, and that it is also the duty of all who have the interests of India at heart to accord them their loyal support.

Mr. Wm. Fowler : A year ago I said a few words, in this room, on this question, on the occasion of the discussion on Mr. Probyn's paper. I recollect very well that Mr. Ralli backed up very warmly, what I then said. Like Mr. Ralli, I wish to speak with the utmost moderation and consideration for the difficulties of the Government of India, at the present moment. There is no doubt, as Sir James Mackay has said, that the action we have now before us is not the accomplishment of the real desire of the Government of India. What they wanted was something different. They wished for a bimetallic arrangement. Now, we are not to discuss bimetallism, and I am not going to discuss it ; but it is important to observe that this is not what the Government of India required. Failing International Bimetallism, they fell back on this idea of the closing of the mints. Now, I believe the figures which Sir Richard Temple has given us go to show that the action of the Indian Government has practically failed ; that is to say, that it has tended to lessen the exports from India and to increase the imports into India, and, so, to diminish the balance of trade in favour of India. Sir Richard Temple has admitted that, I think, in his remarks. The excuse made is, that, although, as Sir

Richard Temple says, the action is unsound, it was necessary. But it is of no use to say it is necessary unless it succeeds. It may be necessary to do a thing if you are sure that that thing is going to bring you the result you intended ; but if it does not bring you the result you intended, how can it be regarded as necessary ? I suppose the idea of the Government was : "We must get more revenue, in London, out of India and so avoid the necessity of borrowing more money in gold." What has been the result ? You have closed the mints, with the consequences to which I have referred and other serious consequences ; but you are still obliged to borrow in gold. They have borrowed two millions on Treasury Bills, and one and a-half million more are advertised for next week, and now we have it announced that an Act of Parliament is to be brought in for a ten million loan. I consider the position to be a very serious one indeed. We were told that when the season of high exchanges came this difficulty would be got over ; that Bills would be sold at a good exchange when the great season of exports in India came, namely, the winter season. The winter season has come, but I understand that no Bills were sold to-day ; very few were sold last Wednesday ; and a comparatively small amount on the previous Wednesday ; and for months before that none were sold. I ask myself what will be the position on 1st April ? We now know the Government will have paid its home charges by borrowing money in England. That will increase the interest charge in gold which the Indian Government have been so anxious to avoid. Now, there is one main point, Sir Richard has hardly referred to, which I think it is very important to consider. When you look forward to the future of India, everybody admits, and everybody knows, that the revenue must be received in silver ; it cannot be received in anything else. You cannot have a gold revenue—at present, at any rate ; and you cannot have a gold revenue until you have a gold standard ; and then, even, you could not change the land settlement and make the natives pay in gold. The revenue must be a revenue in silver. Surely a Government which has such an enormous silver revenue should do all in its power to raise the value of silver and not, by its own action, knock silver down 16 per cent. It seems a most extraordinary position—just the very thing having been done which, in my judgment, the Government ought not to do. It seems to me that to depreciate, by their own act, the value of the revenue they receive is a kind of suicidal action. I remember reading in the report of the committee a very interesting paper by Sir Raymond West, who was an experienced official in India. He says : " I do not care " what you do or say : if you knock down the value of silver, sooner " or later, the Government must feel it in the gold value of the rupee. " You may galvanise the rupee for a short time, but, sooner or later, " the value of the rupee will go down if silver goes down ; so " the Government should avoid injuring the value of silver." To all the arguments which have been used it has been said :—

" We must have money ; if we cannot get it one way we must get "it in another." We have heard about alternatives. I should like to say a word about alternatives. Sir Richard Temple does not seem clear upon the alternative question of his argument. He cannot find alternatives, and therefore he agrees with a proceeding he does not half like. But is there no possibility of economies in India ? I have often been told there is not, but I should like to suggest one I referred to in the House of Commons many years ago, but it was like crying in the wilderness ; I refer to the very large sums which are spent every year out of revenue on public works in India. In England we do not do that. We borrow money, and pay it back over thirty or fifty years, for important permanent works. I remember in the Report Mr. Ralli calculated that in three years India had spent twelve millions out of revenue on permanent works of a public character. It would make a vast difference to India if she had spread that payment over a series of years. I suggest that as a matter of import- ance, and I do not see why a mode of finance which is regarded as sound in England should be regarded as unsound in India. I remember saying this to Sir Grant Duff, and his reply was : " We " cannot trust the officials unless the expenditure is made out of " revenue." Then if you cannot trust them I say the time has come for you to change your officials. Let the officials exercise economy and not force the Government into a mode of finance which must be very unfair to the existing generation of taxpayers. We should not dream of doing it in England. Why do it in India ? I hardly venture to refer to the Army in India ; I suppose it may be said the economy is impossible, but I am not sure that it is. I should like to say a word with reference to a remark made by Sir Richard Temple and by one of the speakers who followed him, with regard to the position of silver in the world. I am one of those who think it is important that we should not assume that silver is to be discarded as money. I think we ought to do all we can to keep both metals in operation. You know I do not approve of bimetallism ; but I say that those who use gold ought to do nothing to discourage silver in other coun- tries ; and we ought not to take action like this which is a deadly blow at the use of silver by one of the largest users of silver in the world. Much as I dislike the idea of bimetallism, I would rather have bimetallism than any attempt to destroy the value of silver. I regard such a step as so dangerous that I would rather have bi- metallism than any such proceeding as this. We must remember too, that when dealing with the position of silver, we have no right to assume that what is going on now is to continue for ever. See what is going on in Africa ! Who shall say that the discoveries of gold will not overtake the discovery of silver before we are many years older. It would not surprise me. I remember saying that before the discoveries of gold in Africa, but now I have more hope than I ever had that I may live to see again what I remember in my boyhood when the great difficulty was that gold was so plentiful that people did not know what to do with it. Now we have seen the reverse happen. I remember a conversation with my father when I was very young, during which I asked : What is going to happen when the sovereign is only worth half-a-sovereign ? His reply to me was : Leave it alone ; it will take care of itself. It has taken care of itself. I am not one of those who believe in what is commonly called the appreciation of gold, but certainly gold has not depreciated. I have listened to this paper with great interest and I have tried to express how utterly I disapprove of the action of the Indian Government ; but I wish to say how heartily I thank Sir Richard Temple for his paper, having regard to his long and great experience as an Indian official.

Mr. L. C. PROBYN : I cannot agree with the remarks made by Mr. Schmidt, as to the complete failure of the plan which has been adopted by the Indian Government. I almost regret that Sir Richard Temple did not lay more stress on the effect which the closing of the mints had on the value of the rupee. That effect has been very often misunderstood by people who ought to have known better. People talk, and some of the leading financial papers talk, as if the intrinsic value of the rupee corresponded at present to its exchange value. Most of you gentlemen in this room know this is not the case ; but I do not think this point has been sufficiently emphasised to-night. At the rate of 32$d$., the present price of silver, the intrinsic value of the rupee is less than 1$s$., and yet its market value as you know is more than 1$s$. 3$d$. This being the case it seems to me quite wrong to say that the Government have met with no success in their scheme. I will go further than Sir Richard Temple. I will say that not only have they met with a modicum of success, but they have met with a considerable amount of success. They have succeeded in fixing the value of the rupee totally independent of its intrinsic value. I think anyone who heard the paper which I read here a year ago, will agree with me in thinking that a very serious mistake was made by the Government in attempting as it did to raise the value of the rupee to 1$s$. 4$d$. What I said in this room was—and I say it again—that it was the greatest possible mistake to attempt to raise the value of the rupee by closing the mints. All that should have been done was to try and keep it at the value of the day ; and I think many will agree with me that if this plan had been adopted—if, instead of a 16$d$. rate, a 15$d$. rate had chosen, we should have had a very different story to tell. I do not despair yet of a 1$s$. 4$d$. rate being made effective, but I do not think the Government has gone the right way to work. I think the Government should have been bolder and have declared its policy with more certainty, and have said that it intended to adopt a gold standard in India at some specified rate. Sir James Mackay was wrong in saying that 1$s$. 4$d$. is fixed by legislative enactment. It is nothing of the kind. It is in the power of the Government to raise the rate from 16*d.* to 18*d.*

Sir James Mackay : I do not think I said that, Mr. Probyn.

Mr. Probyn : Then I beg your pardon. The mistake the Indian Government made was that they did not say what their aim and object was, and that they did not declare their intention to have a gold standard at a certain rate. And then they made another mistake in trying to force up the value of their Council Bills. They could not get a certain price for their Council Bills, and therefore they would not sell them at all. This means a bad piece of policy, and what was the result ? It resulted in the shipment of large quantities of silver to India. I think in the months of July, August and September four millions of tens of rupees of silver were received in India. If the Government had made up its mind to have a gold standard, every ounce of silver which went to India made the achievement more difficult—more impossible. We must not disguise from ourselves that the rupee has now become simply an inconvertible coin with all the characteristics of inconvertible paper money. It was simply impossible that by a *dictum* of the Government the value of the rupee should be fixed at any price. What should determine the value of the rupee is the same principle that determines the value of the paper dollar in Argentina—the state of trade, the amount of rupees in circulation, and the expectation of their redemption. I should like to make a few remarks on that part of the paper in which Sir Richard Temple dealt with the uncoined silver in India. I have always held that the most serious obstacle to the introduction of a gold standard in India was the quantity of uncoined silver in that country. Sir Richard Temple, I think, fixed the uncoined silver at something like 200 millions, but I believe he has very much under estimated it ; I believe the uncoined silver in India is more like 300 millions of tens of rupees. Since Sir Richard was in India, a very careful census has been made by Mr. F. C. Harrison of the quantity of rupees in existence and the conclusions at which he arrives are that the uncoined silver amounts to 300 millions of tens of rupees. Now this uncoined silver has, by the action of the Government been not merely reduced in value 16 per cent., but a good deal more, because the value is now measured not in silver, but in a conventional rupee. Taking silver at 32*d.* per ounce and taking the rupee at 1*s.* 3*d.*, it means this, that there has been a loss on the uncoined silver of nearly 20¾ per cent., and the more you raise the value of the rupee the greater does that apparent loss become. The native will look to the value of the uncoined silver, not in the amount of grain, wheat, or other commodity that he can buy, but to its value against the coined silver ; and if by any possibility the Goverment could raise the token value of the rupee to 1*s.* 6*d.*, there would be an apparent loss to the holder of uncoined silver of 33 per cent. Now this is a very serious matter. I wish that Sir Richard Temple, with his vast experience, had indicated to us what he thought should now be the action of the Government.. I confess myself that the only solution of the difficulty appears to me to be that the Government should at once declare what its policy is, supposing it determines upon having a 16*d.* rupee, to say it intends to have that, no matter at what cost ; that if it be necessary to buy up the currency it will do so, and that if necessary it will go to any expense to make the rupee be an effective gold token. I do not think it is at all necessary, as I said a year ago, that you should have a gold currency in India. I believe the rupee answers the purpose of the people of India perfectly well. All that is wanted is that it should have a good solid gold backing. Mr. Schmidt said a year ago that a gold standard without gold was like a race horse without legs. He is right ; yet that is what some people are aiming at. I say the Government should make up its mind to have a good solid gold basis to its rupees, so that if anyone brought rupees to a place set apart for the purpose, he would be able to exchange rupees into gold just in the same way as a man exchanges a Bank of England Note into sovereigns.

PROFESSOR FOXWELL :—I have noted one or two points upon which I shall be glad to say a few words. Sir Richard Temple himself speaks of the recent action of the Indian Government as " a monetary expedient—unsound in principle "; but he says it is not open to bimetallists to take this view. He does not see how the adherents of the bimetallic theory can consistently object to the appreciation of the rupee. In reply to this challenge, I would say that there is a sense in which the principle of the Act is undoubtedly sound. Let us imagine that the currency of India consisted of inconvertible paper, and that this paper, by over-issue or otherwise, had become depreciated in reference to gold, or whatever other standard of comparison had been adopted. Everyone will admit that its value could be raised by restricting its issue, and that such a course would be a proper one to take. But we may allow that the principle of raising value by limitation of quantity is sound, and yet object *in toto* to the particular application of it in this Indian Currency Act. What we object to in the present scheme, from this point of view, is, that you are dealing with a metallic currency in such a way as to cause a severance between the bullion and the monetary value of the metal. You cannot sever the metallic and the mintage values of a legal tender metal, without exposing your currency to grave dangers ; and we have never approved and entirely deprecate any such policy, as being artificial, arbitrary, and unstable. Again, bimetallism might be shortly described as a protest against an appreciation of gold brought about by a demoneti- sation of silver. How then can bimetallists fail to disapprove a scheme which not only nails the rupee to the sovereign so that its value must henceforth follow the appreciating value of gold, but actually does this in such a way as to increase the tendency of gold to appreciate ? The aim of bimetallists has always been to increase the stability of money. They cannot approve a highly artificial scheme, the first effect of which is to make the rupee as unstable in value as the sovereign, and the second to increase the instability of the sovereign itself. The bimetallists then are perfectly consistent in condemning the policy of the Indian Act, the dangers of which they were among the first to point out before its adoption. If there is one gentleman in this room to-night who has a right to feel a certain self-satisfaction, it is Mr. Hermann Schmidt. It is not every one, who, having had the courage to make a very definite forecast upon a very complicated and difficult question, has the good fortune to find that forecast verified to the letter within something like a year from the time when it was made. It will be remembered by many now present, that Mr. Schmidt, in some able letters to *The Times*, and afterwards in this room, and in a remarkable pamphlet, pointed out that the then suggested policy was exposed to serious dangers—to danger of forgery and alternative remittance, and to danger of a reversal of the Indian balance of trade. These warnings of Mr. Schmidt have been verified in a degree which even he can hardly have anticipated. Short as the time is which has elapsed since the passing of the Act, it is clear that the Act has broken down exactly at the points he indicated. The Government hoped that by controlling the issue of rupees, the Indian legal tender, they would practically control remittance, and therefore the rate of exchange. It is now clear that there has been a leakage somewhere. In some way or other alternative forms of remittance have been found. No doubt rupees outside India have been bought up by the exchange banks. Again, there has been an enormous import of silver into India, only twice exceeded (in the exceptional years 1890 and 1892). I am told by a leading bullion broker that this silver has gone largely into Native States. It may be that this points to irregular mintage in some form or other. Or it may be, again, that the native up-country, innocent of what has been done at Calcutta, is induced by dealers to accept the weight of silver in the rupee, or a little more than this weight, as equivalent to the rupee, as it really was equivalent before the passing of the Act. One thing is certain. Remittance in rupees has been successfully evaded, there has, consequently, been no demand for Council Bills at a price higher than that of the alternative modes of remittance, and the whole operation has got out of hand. But, it is said, this difficulty is temporary. It may be granted, though it is not certain, that the present facilities for alternative remittance may ultimately diminish. But then we are brought face to face with a more serious and fundamental question. Will the balance of remittance continue to be in favour of India, as has been the case hitherto ? Here the latest statistics, which Sir Richard Temple has kindly supplied, are extremely significant. They show that the effect of the Act, by increasing India's imports on the one hand, and by diminishing her exports on the other, has been to entirely reverse the balance of trade. For nearly three hundred years that balance has been in favour of India. India has been a sink into which the precious metals have flowed, never to return. It looks as if the stream might now be reversed. In that case the present Act, unless supplemented by some new measure, must break down. Sir James Mackay, it is true, regards this reversal of the balance of trade as a temporary affair, incidental to the introduction of the scheme. If this were really so, we might perhaps look with more complacency on the proposed £10,000,000 sterling loan. It would merely represent the price India had to pay for the blunders committed in connection with the Act, which, by general consent, was introduced at the worst possible season of the year, and without adequate safeguards. But I see no reason to take this view. The circumstances which have reversed the balance of trade are not temporary ones. They are of the essence of the new policy, and their influence tends rather to increase as time goes on. As Mr. Schmidt pointed out a year ago, the Act first arrests the fall in the gold value of the rupee, and so enables Manchester and other goods to enter Indian markets on more favourable terms, it being unlikely that rupee prices will be proportionately lowered; and secondly, the artificial appreciation of the rupee above its value as silver has diminished the power of Indian exports to compete in the markets of the silver-using countries of the Far East. Thus imports are increased, exports diminished; and this is no mere hypothesis, for the reasoning is exactly borne out by the events. The import of Manchester goods has greatly increased, while the export of opium and Indian yarns and piece goods has greatly diminished. The establishment of cotton mills takes time, but there is little doubt that Japan will soon be ousting Bombay from the Eastern markets: and already a considerable stimulus has been given to Japanese exports of coal. We do not seem to be justified, then, in assuming that the balance of trade will recover itself, but rather that it will go from bad to worse. To meet such a condition of things by a succession of sterling loans would clearly be impossible. Even if it were not deplorable finance, it would have the effect of saddling India with an increasing gold debt, and thereby increasing the very burden of gold remittance which it was a main purpose of the Act to reduce. In the objections I have so far raised to the Act, I have regarded it merely from the Anglo-Indian standpoint, as a scheme for dealing with an Anglo-Indian difficulty; and I do not think that any wider considerations can have been in the minds of those who forced this policy on the Government of India. But we are bound to look at the whole matter from a broader point of view. When we do so, the fundamental defect of the new Indian policy is obvious. It is an attempt to make a parochial settlement of what is really a great international question. You cannot isolate India and consider her monetary difficulties apart from the general monetary situation which has caused them. The attempt to do so is the real cause of the failure of the Act. I must ask leave for a moment, to point out precisely what this monetary situation is, because expressions are constantly used, and some have been heard to-night, which seem to show an absence of clearness as to the facts. We are all extremely indebted to Sir Richard Temple for the lucid, concise, and comprehensive way in which he has laid before us the various topics suggested by the Indian Act. But, perhaps, he did not enlarge as fully as he might have done upon the exact nature of the evils the Act was intended to meet. He spoke frequently of the depreciation of silver. Now I do not suppose, for a moment, that that term misled him, but it might possibly confuse some of those who are not so familiar with the subject. What are the facts? There has been a depreciation, no doubt, in the gold value of silver, but not in its real value. Its value in commodities has remained almost unaltered. Sir Richard, himself, has furnished us with a proof of this in the paper. He has observed very truly that the gold-price of silver has fallen about 37 per cent. since 1873. Now that figure represents, within a fraction, the average fall in the gold-price of commodities over the same period. It follows that the relation between silver and commodities is unchanged. The great change has been in gold. The ruling factor in the recent monetary troubles has been the appreciation of gold ; the so-called depreciation of the rupee not being a real depreciation, but only a fall in its gold value. Mr. William Fowler tells us he does not believe in the appreciation of gold. The difference between us must, I think, be mainly one of terms ; for the facts are really beyond dispute. It has been established by leading statists in all countries—by extreme monometallists like Mr. Giffen, and moderate ones like Soetbeer, as well as by writers on the other side—that the gold prices of wholesale commodities have fallen some 35 per cent. below the average level during the period 1853—77, or, put the same fact inversely, that the purchasing power of the sovereign in 1892 is about 50 per cent. more than it was on the average of those 25 years, the purchasing power of silver remaining about what it was in 1873. It follows that the exchange between gold and silver currencies must have fluctuated considerably, and in these two disturbances, the appreciation of gold, and the fluctuation of exchange, we have the real sources of our monetary troubles. Looked at from this point of view, the remedy forced upon India by the Home Government appears to me grotesque in its incongruity. At the best (that is, if it does not break down), it only steadies the exchange between India and gold countries, at the cost of unsettling it, as between India and silver countries ; and it does this in such a way as to still further disturb the exchange between gold and non-rupee silver countries, while, worst of all, it must promote the further demonetisation of silver, and so aggravate the appreciation of gold, which is the great obstacle to the revival of trade. If I may use a homely illustration, it is as if there were two express trains, timed to arrive within five minutes of one another. The second train is half an hour late, and to put matters in order, some worthy official decides to delay the first express half an hour also, instead of bringing the second up to time. I will only add in conclusion, that I have not intended in anything I have said, to reflect on the action of the Indian Government. I think the scheme they adopted a dangerous one ; but, we must remember, it was not the one they desired ; and I for one, think that with all its defects, it was to be preferred to a policy of *laissez faire.* The Indian Government was placed in a very difficult position. Told, as they were by men in responsible positions at home, that gold was the only possible monetary standard ; that silver must be regarded as a base metal, and must be left, unsteadied by monetary use among civilised nations, to take its chance in the market, like copper or tin, the Indian Government were clearly right in demanding that they should be allowed to adopt some better accredited standard. They had on this showing, either to cut themselves adrift from silver or from civilisation. The Home Government gave no reason to hope that England's influence would be exerted to maintain the monetary position of silver ; and, that being so, it was clearly improper for India to maintain the silver standard. The blame must lie with those who restricted the alternatives. It is impossible not to endorse the protest of Mr. Leonard Courtney against the narrowness of the reference to the Indian Currency Committee. But we are told, the Indian Government might have adopted a gold currency as well as a gold standard, for that is what some of the hints thrown out this evening seem to amount to. But is it seriously suggested that such a proposal would have been tolerated by this country ? Could the London market have contemplated with equanimity the necessary withdrawals of gold ? Could India, indeed, have obtained the gold ? She might have placed sterling loans in London ; but as the Austrian example shows, it is one thing to issue a loan, another to get your gold. I agree, then, with Sir Richard Temple that the Indian Government chose the best alternative open to them, precluded as they were from securing a radical and statesmanlike settlement of the question. On the other hand, I agree that the measure adopted is a very defective one. Even from the parochial point of view it is fraught with dangers, and may prove a complete failure ; from the international point of view, its absurdity is patent, as it directly aggravates the root of all the mischief. But I have always thought that the measure, with all its defects, defects which could not have been altogether overlooked by the Indian Government, would have one beneficial result. I felt sure that it would inevitably, as its results developed themselves, oblige the Home Government to treat the monetary question seriously, and probably commit them in the end to the policy of international arrangement, the only final and comprehensive solution. This result may, perhaps, have been in the minds of some of those, who, with many misgivings, finally decided to close the mints. At any rate, the authors of the measure may urge in its justification that it will strengthen the hands of the British Government if the occasion for any international negotiations should arise.

Mr. HERBERT GIBBS : I have very little to add to what Professor Foxwell has said, but I might perhaps remind him that the ten millions that the Indian Government want on this occasion is not ten millions in gold to be shipped, but merely ten millions to be raised here to pay their indebtedness in this country. Therefore, no gold will be required. That is so ?

SIR RICHARD TEMPLE : Yes.

Mr. HERBERT GIBBS : Though I have very little to say, I should like to emphasize more than has been done, the disastrous nature of the alternative that the Indian Government is reduced to. Sir Richard Temple admits, or rather insists, that it is objectionable in principle ; but I do not think anyone has pointed out how objectionable it is. The present position, Mr. Probyn says, is that the Government have been successful. To parody the expression of a great general, " if they go on succeeding much longer they will be ruined." They passed this law a few months ago closing the mints and now they have to come to this Government for authority to raise ten millions—what for ? To meet the current expenditure—to meet the expenditure of the year. A great many people in defending the Indian Government have said that this is an experiment. Sir Richard Temple however, knows that it is not an experiment, and anyone who has read about the difficulties of the various Governments with which we are very familiar in this city, knows that it is an expedient which has been tried over and over again and has failed. The Indian Government have not indeed issued paper but none the less, they have instituted a forced currency in order to try and pay their way. That is the first step that a South American Government takes, only they issue paper and with that paper they endeavour to pay their way. South American Governments being more versed in financial expedients than the Indian Government, are able to carry on for some time before they come to the English market for a loan to raise the exchange and meet their current expenditure. The Indian Government apparently, directly after they have adopted the first expedient are obliged to adopt the second expedient of coming to the English market for a loan, " to raise the exchange and to meet their current expenditure." I do not know how many times I have heard that expression, but never before in connection with any Government under the control of the English nation. Is this an experiment ? In one sense it is. It is an experiment for a great dependency of England to adopt the financial expedients of South America. Several speakers have referred to this question but they seem to shrink from an ugly word ; there is, however, no doubt in the world that if the Government of India continue in this course, and if the balance of expenditure and revenue does not alter for the better, the Indian Government must become bankrupt. "Surely," says Sir Richard, " in monetary and financial crises the Governments in other countries have taken steps not strictly justifiable in principle." Surely they have ; but, with what results ! As we are debarred from speaking about bimetallism, which is the only practical remedy that I know of, there is nothing for me to do except to insist so far as I can upon the disastrous alternatives that the Government of India has adopted.

Mr. ROBERT BARCLAY (Manchester): At this late hour it is scarcely necessary that I should take any part in this debate, especially as I think the main points have already been very fully and ably gone into. I join in the expression of thanks to Sir Richard Temple for the able and clear statement he has made as to this measure. The Indian Government got power to carry it out, and were recommended to do so by a certain Committee. The Committee took a large amount of evidence, and I hold—and many who have read that evidence also hold—that the counsel which the Committee gave to the Indian Government was totally against the weight of the evidence taken by it. Taking into account all the various views and opinions set before that Committee, no one can justify the advice which it gave. The Indian Government were in a fix, and, as you have heard, the whole thing is attempted to be justified only upon the ground of necessity, in view of revenue and expenditure. Well, to tamper with the currency of a country—because it really comes to that—for the sake of increasing the revenue, or to make it go further, is just doing what the old Tudors did when they debased the currency of England to bring about the same effect—that is, to make the revenue go further. The whole course of this debate has brought out the inherent weakness of any system which can be brought forward to meet the case apart from the one real remedy which the Indian Government wanted. We are here not to debate that remedy, however, therefore we cannot do so ; but the whole debate has been in favour of bimetallism by the process of exhaustion. No other plan to meet the case effectually can be proposed. I was very much amused when Mr. Fowler began with his alternative remedies. The only one that he mentioned was that the Indian Government should economise. Now does any gentleman with any knowledge of India believe that economy in any or all departments would have met this great difficulty. It is utterly impossible. Then again, what Mr. Fowler said to-night, otherwise, is very valuable to the bimetallic cause. The Indian Government were forced, as he expresses it, to enter upon this scheme, by the determination that England would have nothing to do with bi-metallism. He is one of the foremost of monometallists, yet he confesses that if he had realised what the Government of India were going to do, he would rather that bimetallism had been established. That is a very important confession. Then we have heard from him that silver is not to be set aside. Silver must enter into the currencies of the world. It is there, and you must deal with it, and, therefore, to deal with the matter in a *parochial* way, as Prof. Foxwell has just said, is nonsense. You are trying to control something in a given area, which is affected by all surrounding areas, and it is utterly impossible to bring about any suitable settlement in this way.

Mr. JOHN DUN : As the hour is late, I will make but a very few brief remarks. My own impression in this matter is that we are a little too premature in judging of the results of the important step which the Council of India took in June last. I think we must give the policy reasonable time to work itself out in its own way. Perhaps the result may be as those who oppose it seem to consider—a disastrous result. For my own part, I think and hope that it will not be so. There is one thing that this measure of the Indian Government has unquestionably done—it has prevented a fall in the exchange which would otherwise most probably have taken place upon the enormous fall that took place in the value of silver. It has steadied the exchanges which is much and which is one of the main points—the very main point which the measure was designed to secure. That this measure will stand the test of the future is what nobody can predict because nobody can possibly predict what will be the future of silver. The future of silver may be an oscillation with very slight variations round something like the present level. The future of silver may on the other hand be a very considerable further depreciation on the present gold price of silver, or the gold price of silver may in the future—not in the immediate future, but in a more remote future which most of us may live to see—rise ; and rise considerably, and it will be necessary to consider—and this is a point Sir Richard Temple abstained from dealing with—how this scheme is to work in the future under those contingencies. Of course we need not say anything about the contingency of a continuance of the present value of silver ; but let us take the contingency of a further fall in the price of silver. It will surely be a very difficult matter without a gold circulation and without a gold reserve to maintain the over-valued silver coinage at the par or at anything nearly approaching to the par, of 1s. 4d. for the rupee. Then again, we we must look forward to the possibility, one which I think is a very great possibility, and a stronger possibility than the other, that permanently we may have in future years a very great rise in the gold price of silver. Those causes likely to contribute to that rise are perfectly evident. In the first place, the shutting down of mines which are at present unprofitable, thereby diminishing supply ; in the second place, the increased use of silver in the arts in consequence of its diminished price, thereby increasing demand ; and thirdly, lastly, and chiefly, the augmentation which seems to be setting in very strongly in the annual production of gold. Now, how will this policy of the Indian Government stand the test of a rise in the gold price of silver? Instead of being an over-valued coin, the rupee will become an under-valued coin ; therefore, the rupee will tend, under the action of the Gresham law, to leave India, and its place would be taken by gold. Will gold under those circumstances pour with sufficient rapidity into India in order to take the place of silver, not only as the standard of value with a reserve but also as a circulating currency? And it is intended to give India an actual gold circulation in the future. That is a very difficult question, as to the practicability of which I am not in a position to speak; I can foresee that in the future there will be between the present position of affairs—namely, an over valued silver currency which is nevertheless legal tender to an unlimited amount— and the transition to an undervalued subsidiary silver currency, with a gold currency circulating and backed by a gold reserve. The progress from the present position to that future position seems to be fraught with an enormous amount of difficulty in the practical working of the currency of India, and a difficulty also to the finances of India ; and it seems to me I almost discern in the future —although I yield to nobody in my feelings as to the unscientific character of bimetallism—that if we are to establish a gold currency in India with a subsidiary silver currency—which seems to be the present policy—we may have to wade through the mire of bimetallism in order to attain that result.

Sir Richard Temple (In reply) : On considering the report of the speeches made in the discussion which followed upon the reading of my paper, I do not feel that I have any particular rejoinder to make to the criticisms offered by most, though not all, of the speakers,—which criticisms are destructive rather than constructive. The objections to the action of the Government of India have been effectively stated—I have never denied these, nor do I now deny them. The closing of the mints was only an unavoidable experiment of which the success or failure has yet to be determined. My defence was moderate, guarded, and stated with all reserve. The Institute of Bankers will, I hope, consider my defence of the action of the Government, I do not think it can be put stronger. They will read what is said against it, and they must judge whether it is sufficient or not.

But the discussion confirms what I stated in my paper, namely this, that the objectors can offer no alternative action, save one, namely—Bimetallism. Yet they make no attempt to show how Bimetallism could be introduced by India which must be in conjunction with England—nor how England, or the City of London, could be got to agree—nor how, if they did agree, the rest of the world could be brought into the line of concurrence—nor how Bimetallism could be introduced into the British Empire without the concurrence of the rest of the world.

Of course they may say that the Government of India could have refrained from action altogether. Well, let the Institute of Bankers consider the situation of the Government as sketched in my paper, and say whether the Government could have been expected to remain inactive.

No doubt the failure to sell Council Bills at an acceptable rate, the temporary reversal of the balance of trade, the necessity for raising a temporary gold loan in London, do afford several handles to objectors. I admit that these difficulties do, in part, arise from the action of the Government, and I must make the objectors a present of that argument. But I contend that they have arisen in part, certainly, and perhaps principally, from physical and material causes apart from silver. The question is whether, during the early months of the coming year, the Indian exports will exceed the imports in value, as has, heretofore, proved to be the case. We hope they will—if they do, then the difficulty regarding the Council Bills may pass away. If they do not, then, no doubt, the monetary position will have to be re-considered. Meanwhile, I contend that the Government, by raising the temporary gold loan in London, are quite right in giving the experiment a fair trial, in shielding it from disadvantages which may prove to be owing to other causes and to separate circumstances, in affording it a chance of proving its efficacy. Some months must elapse before its efficacy, or inefficacy can be determined.